REMEMBER MY NAME

Erkut Sogut

First published in Great Britain in 2022, by CA Publishing House Ltd

Typesetting by Tom Witcomb
Cover Design by Nick Castle

ISBN 978-1-7397288-4-7 (papberback)

CA Publishing House
Summit House,170 Finchley Road
London, United Kingdom
NW3 6BP

www.erkutsogut.com

Dedicated to my beloved mother and father.

ALSO BY ERKUT SOGUT

Deadline

Prologue

Isaac stood leaning on the bonnet of the van. He casually scanned the horizon, thinking of their next steps. It didn't matter that they had killed the guy; the death of an immigrant in a run-down area was not top of the Paris police's priority list. All they had to do was make sure they properly covered their tracks, lie low for a few days and soon enough someone would file away the case as just another case of immigrant-on-immigrant crime. No doubt there would be those who said he probably deserved it. You didn't get into those situations unless you knew those sorts of people. Little did they know.

'Come on, we've waited around here too long,' he said to 'Patou', and moved to the front passenger side of the battered, black VW Transporter. The nickname came from the casual term they gave to guard dogs in the mountains. Farmers used them to protect livestock from bears and wolves. Unlike Leye, Patou and Snoop had been with Isaac for years. He trusted them. For now. There was a commotion inside the rear of the van, but left Snoop to deal with it as his phone buzzed in his pocket.

'Yeah,' Isaac started. He knew who it was. Only one person had the number. Ousman.

'I need you to pick someone up. A woman,' came the reply. He hated talking to Ousman. Tried to make every conversation as swift as possible. The man oozed violence. It came out in every syllable he spoke. But he much preferred to talk to him on the phone. In person, you were at the mercy of his temper. Isaac had seen it in action. It's how he'd ended up with the job.

'Which one?'

'The journalist that's been talking to your Boy Wonder. She's ruffling a lot of feathers. She'll be at a cafe in the city, near Père-Lachaise. I'll text you the address. I want her gone. But keep the kid around.'

'Sure. Ten minutes,' Isaac said, and hung up. He breathed a brief sigh of relief, shook off the uncomfortable feeling that had crept over him as he spoke to Ousman. He turned to the back of the van.

'New job, boys. Ousman wants us to pick someone up.'

'That prick, what are we, a taxi service for his whores?' came the response.

'Not that kind of pick up, moron. Some woman refusing to wind her neck in. Wants us to shut her up. Come on, less talk, more action. Let's go.'

The van's engine roared to life and they moved off to join the highway back into the city. Whilst Isaac hated talking to Ousman, he always gave him good work, the sort of work he enjoyed. Extortion, kidnap, even the odd murder. From an early age, Isaac had always been able to do the dirty work. He only had one rule — no kids.

Today had been a good day, getting Boy Wonder under their wing, in their pocket. The case would go cold, but he'd always know that they knew he was there. That they could implicate him and bring his entire career tumbling down. He'd be no good on jobs, too goody-two-shoes for that sort of stuff. But they could make sure they took their cut for the foreseeable. And the higher he went, the bigger that cut got. For now, though, they needed him to keep quiet. Kid had a hero complex.

'Leye,' Isaac shouted over the racket in the back of the van, 'Bag him.'

He turned and watched the boy wrap his friend's head in one of the black burlap sacks they'd brought. Now that kid was dangerous. Nothing seemed to faze him. He did anything you said. Would need a tight leash, though.

The Boy Wonder bucked and struggled against his friend, and Isaac could hear the rapid panting. He decided to fuck with the kid. Told him to be careful who he associated with.

'This lady journalist is dangerous to know.'

He saw Leye murmur something in his friend's ear and he seemed to relax. It made it easier for Leye to connect the pistol to the side of his head, landing a vicious overhand strike that sent the kid to the floor.

'Come on,' Isaac said to Patou. 'Put your foot down. We've got work to do.'

They pulled into the fast lane and back into the melee of the city.

* * *

'Pull up here,' Isaac ordered Patou as they pulled onto the street Ousman had directed them to in his message. Rain lashed the windscreen. He checked the picture that had come through as well and craned his neck to look through the glass, scanning the pavement ahead for the journalist. There was no sign of her, but Isaac had a full view of the cafe she was meant to be in.

'Leye, go check she's still in there,' Isaac commanded, 'Here, take a look.' Keeping his eyes glued to the street, he passed his phone back to Leye and heard the van door slide open and watched as he made his way down the street. Leye walked past the window, casting a furtive glance inside, then pulled up just beyond and checked the picture on the phone. After a few moments, he left his spot and moved back towards where they had parked, checking through the window again with the slightest movement of his head. He looked up at Isaac and gave a curt nod before settling into a doorway next to the cafe to take shelter from the storm.

No sooner had he settled down than the journalist appeared outside, digging an umbrella out of her bag.

'Okay, that's her. Let's go,' Isaac said, unclipping his seat belt and climbing into the back.

Patou pulled away from the kerb at speed and they were outside the cafe before they knew it.

'Go,' Patou said as he slammed on the brakes.

In one fluid motion, Isaac slid the door open and he and Snoop erupted out of the rear of the vehicle. With an agility that defied his gangly frame, Snoop got behind the woman and grabbed one of her arms and a handful of hair before pushing her towards the van. She struggled, bringing the umbrella down on his head, but Leye emerged from his hiding spot and took hold of her other arm. The rain was keeping people off of the streets. There was no one to stop them. Isaac reached into his jacket pocket for another hood and pulled it tight around the woman's head, cinching it at the back.

The three men bundled the journalist inside the van, where she sprawled out on the floor next to Boy Wonder. Fitting, thought Isaac briefly, as he saw the two laid out before him. The door slammed shut behind him and the van lurched forward, throwing him off balance. He steadied himself and watched as the journalist groped around in the dark before pulling out his gun and delivering a stunning blow to the side of her head. He smiled to himself as she slumped down again, sinking into oblivion.

'To the warehouses,' he said. 'It's the weekend. No one will find her for days.'

I

Annabel alighted the train carriage and worked her way through the crowd towards the exit, twisting her rucksack to the front of her body, unconsciously hugging it, her hands protecting the zips and pockets.

She passed a group of teenagers sitting in a makeshift circle, perched on rucksacks almost as big as they were and felt a slight pang of regret that she had missed her opportunity for inter-railing, travelling to the furthest corners of the globe. She'd had to work. She made her mark in a different way.

Annabel joined the queue to move through customs and couldn't avoid feeling flushed when the guard spent what felt like an age assessing the VISA stamps in the back of her passport. She had travelled, then; she consoled herself. She doubted any kids she'd walked past would ever set foot in some of the places she had. Perhaps they'd never want to.

She walked through the Gare du Nord, past the rows of shops and eateries packed with couples on romantic getaways, more travelling teenagers uniformed in harem pants and sandals, commuters trying to ignore them all and pick up a quick bite before trudging to the office.

Outside it was a clear day, the morning air was crisp, and Annabel walked past the rank of taxis as North African men tried in vain to hustle her inside their waiting cars. Cities were for walking through, and she had a few hours to kill before her meeting.

She made her way down the wide boulevards and noted how different they made the city feel. London was closed in. Cars, people, buses packed onto tiny streets, winding around giant high rises. In Paris, you could see the sky. People could pass one another without having to perform an elaborate, vaguely aggressive dance. Bikes rode separately to the traffic. It was busy, but it felt different. She began to daydream again of getting out of the city where she had grown up. But something kept her there. She didn't subscribe to Johnson's adage that 'a man who is tired of London is tired of life...' but there was something in it. She fed off of the energy of her home city .

As she reached the centre of Paris, Annabel detoured from the main boulevard onto a side street stopped off at a boulangerie. She sat at a table outside, and soon a waiter made his way to her table.

'Bonjour, madame. Je vous écoute?'

He gave her a pleasant smile. Annabel wasn't sure where the stereotype of rude Parisian servers came from. There were many things she didn't like about the city, but it was something she'd never encountered. She imagined there was a strong correlation between those customers who had found the servers rude and the servers finding those customers rude.

'*Bonjour...*' Annabel racked her brain for her limited French vocabulary, '*Un petit pan, et un cafe, s'il vous plaît.*' She didn't even really like pain-au-chocolat, but it was one of the few things she felt comfortable ordering. The other was wine, but she didn't think it was appropriate to order a glass, given the time of day.

The waiter turned and walked into the restaurant, returning a few moments later with an espresso and a warm pastry that flaked as

Annabel took a bite. Rich aromas of butter and chocolate wafted to her nostrils, the sweetness hitting her tongue. The coffee was awful—bitter, thick. Since working in a coffee shop when she was studying, she had developed a snobbishness around her coffee. But this wasn't designed to be sipped. It was classic espresso — a quick caffeine kick intended to be knocked back before getting on with the day.

Annabel finished her breakfast and was relieved when the waiter brought her bill to the table without having to dredge up more high-school French. *L'addition, I think?* She left the money, with a tip, on the saucer and set off again towards the Seine. As a Londoner, she had grown up understanding that rivers formed the lifeblood of a city. The rivers had been there for millennia. They had birthed the communities that had sprung up on their banks and would outlive them. Annabel checked her bag, ticking off the contents on a mental list. She was travelling light, with just her Dictaphone, laptop and notepad. She got up, gave a quick *au revoir* to the waiter, and moved back onto the main drag and down towards the water.

* * *

Having spent the morning surrounded by the city's grand buildings, the difference out in the *banlieue* was stark. Things weren't run down, though Annabel was sure she'd be able to find 'no go' areas not too far away. The architecture was flatter — right-angled and drab grey, the occasional pop of colour where a flag hung or flowerpots adorned the balconies of apartment blocks. The only Chanel here was on the replica handbags a group of teenage girls carried as they bustled past her, chatting animatedly. iPhones glued to their hands, they live-streamed their walk down the street, posing for selfies in a seamless flow, never breaking stride.

Annabel's cab pulled into the ground, and she handed over her fare, remembering to ask for a receipt. Annabel smiled as she noted the cars in the parking lot. A few Mercedes that she was sure the owners would describe as vintage, but were just past their sell-by date. A relatively new VW Golf, which she presumed was the manager's, and an alarming amount of white vans. She wondered how many of these belonged to the players — the club paid its players salaries, but many of them augmented these with regular jobs. She marveled at how a club whose youth program had given rise to several international players could look so down on its luck.

Her contact was waiting for her, propping open the door to the clubhouse.

'Annabel, great to see you again! Thank you for coming all this way.' Moussa's smile stretched from ear to ear as he reached out to embrace her, planting a kiss on each cheek. 'Can I get you anything to drink? The coffee is terrible, but it's after twelve, and the bar is stocked....'

It was Annabel who smiled then, 'Moussa, I don't know what you've heard about journalists, but we're not all complete lushes. I'd take a Coke or something, though?'

Annabel unpacked her things from her bag as Moussa made a show of pouring the soda. Ice in the glass, a lime wedge. 'Football's gain is barkeeping's loss, Moussa,' she joked as he came back over to the table where she'd set up her things.

'*Madame*,' he continued the joke, wearing it a little too thin.

'*Merci*,' Annabel took a sip and placed the drink away from her Dictaphone. She'd lost one too many pieces of equipment to spills.

'We are on the record already? You don't waste time,' Moussa raised a conspiratorial eyebrow.

'We're not talking about scandal today — you shouldn't have anything to worry about, should you?' Annabel shot back.

She liked Moussa, felt comfortable with the teasing, comfortable enough to tease back. The truth was that she knew Moussa was a golden child. There were no flies on him. He'd come up through the academy and had a promising start to his career. He'd even had a call-up for the French international squad, though he never got off the bench. But he had been cursed by injury. Lightning quick down the wing, his blessing had also been his curse as he became a target for defenders unafraid to make crunching tackles and take the potential cards. After several operations, he found himself a free agent and had trickled down the leagues — at one point he'd played for a lower league team in the north of England for a couple of years — before landing at the club. He no longer played but had joined the coaching staff and was the frontman for their new initiative to help promising immigrant players find jobs inside and outside of football.

'So, Moussa, tell me — what does this mean to you? Why now?'

'You know a bit about me, right, Annabel? I grew up on these streets. I know how hard it is to make something of yourself. My dad was a painter and decorator. My mum didn't work — she looked after us kids. If it wasn't for football, I'd be doing the same. Or worse. There's a lot of poverty in the suburbs. People who live in the city don't realise it. There are massive, systemic difficulties to overcome. It's gotten better since the riots, but it's still not great. There's a little more money coming in, a few more police, but in Seine-Saint-Denis — ninety-three, as we call it — over twenty-five-per cent of people live below the breadline. The national average is fifteen per cent. Unemployment is over ten per cent, and the only jobs available are cleaning and labouring jobs. It's worse amongst ethnic minorities. These kids, Annabel, have nothing to do. They think no one cares about them, so why should they care?'

'All well and good, Moussa, but how does football come into it?'

'You've seen Parc de Princes — the amount of money that passes through those gates each week is insane. Seven hundred million euros a year. The pandemic stung everyone, and the clubs are posting losses, as though they're in the same position as Albert, who had to close his bakery. But the profits are crazy. That's supposed to trickle down. They have academies. They have outreach programs. But they can only help so many. But here, we're not just focusing on getting promising players onto the pitch — we're giving them something to do other than that. Helping them find work, stay in school, do better. Sure, some get trials and get sniffs from the bigger clubs, but it's not really about that for us. For me. It's about looking after our communities, getting our kids off the streets and out of the backs of cop cars. This country is amazing, really. It has so much to offer, but you'll never find it if you don't know where to look. We're helping the kids find it.'

'And so it's up and running? Any success stories yet?'

'I'm so glad you asked, Annabel. Hang on...' Moussa delivered the line with practised charm, got up from his seat and went over to the door that led through to the stadium grounds. 'Hey man, are you good? Thanks for doing this.'

As Moussa turned back into the room, a young man, not even in his twenties, followed him in. He was lean, with the sort of frame that no amount of training could achieve. It came through a lifetime of hard labour, of less food than he needed.

'Annabel, this is Afam; Afam, Annabel. She's nice. Mostly,' Moussa pulled out the chair he'd perched on and proffered it to Afam. 'I'll leave you to it. I have a few things I need to do. Text me when you're done, and I'll come back to show you out.'

* * *

Afam shifted in his seat, and Annabel sensed a crack in the cool exterior he'd shown in front of Moussa. This was probably his first time talking to a journalist, she thought.

'Thanks so much for meeting me. Do you mind if we speak English? My French isn't up to much.' She smiled, trying to ease any awkwardness. Afam nodded. 'So, how long have you been at the club?'

Afam considered his answer, his eyes not quite meeting Annabel's, searching up into the corner of the ceiling, 'A few months now. Moussa's a good man. Gave me a chance.'

'And it looks like you've really taken the opportunity and run with it?' she took a sip of her drink, tried to make eye contact again to show him he could trust her.

'Compared to back home, no job they could give me here would be worse.' Afam smiled to himself. 'I used to collect plastic bottles for a living. Go round to store holders and houses and take big sacks of bottles to the recycling centre. It's big business in Lagos. We have a big problem with litter in Nigeria. Lots of plastic. It's better here in Paris, but it shocked me how dirty it is here. Around the tourist attractions it's nice, but only a few streets away there's stuff everywhere. It's like the council has tried to sweep it all under the rug.'

'So, that's home, is it? Lagos? Is there anyone you've left behind? Do you keep in touch with them? I bet you miss it?'

Afam's smile broadened.

'Yes, Lagos. Nigeria is a beautiful country. Lagos is an exciting city. It's not like Paris. It's loud. It's a party town. There is always something happening. I grew up in Ajegunle, AJ City. It's me and my mom, my sister Iman and my two brothers, Azi and Ade. They're twins, not in school yet. They keep my mom very busy. I don't know where my dad went. He was around when we were little, but then just didn't come home one day. Mom said he went to find work, but he could be dead for all I know. He drank a lot.'

'Your sister... she's younger than you?' Annabel avoided the comment about his dad. She wanted to keep this light. She had to fight back the instinct to go for the bigger story. The fallout from the story about nepotism and the Anaia brothers had caused her no end of grief. The heads of clubs had called her editor and made sure he knew Annabel wasn't welcome at press conferences for the foreseeable, which is how she'd been commissioned to write this piece on the scheme at the club. St-Ouen wasn't one of the poverty-stricken boroughs Moussa had spoken about, but it lacked the glamour of its near neighbour. It was a working-class community, with strong historical ties to the left wing, and the club was actively involved in giving back to the community who supported it, in the same way as St Pauli in Hamburg or Livorno in Tuscany.

'She is, yes. My little sister, Iman. She's not so little now, though, I suppose.' Afam's eyes lost their glimmer. His focus waned as he recalled his family.

'You're close to her?'

'Very,' Afam took a deep breath, exhaled, 'When dad left, I had to stop going to school because we needed the money. Iman, she's the bookworm, — she's the one who will do so much good. Who will lift the family up? Everything I do, it's for her.'

'But you're doing good work here as well, Afam? Moussa tells me you're doing great work with the grounds team. Even if the football doesn't work out, you'll have a job to fall back on. A skill, a trade. But from what I hear, that won't be a problem either! Do you get to speak to her? Iman?'

'The first thing I did when I got paid was send an iPad back home for her so we could FaceTime. I top up her SIM, or she goes to the library in the city where she has Wi-Fi, and I help her with her homework, though she's smarter than me. I mainly just sit with her and chat. But anyway, that's another story for another time — you're not here to talk to me about my family!' Afam's attention drew back into the room, and he became animated.

They talked solidly for the next hour, Afam describing how he'd been scouted at an academy back home. He had performed at trials, been shortlisted as a promising young talent, and selected for trials at a sister club in Paris. They had arranged everything, though he'd had to fund the travel himself. His family, his neighbours, had scrimped together the money for his airfare, and eventually he had landed at Charles de Gaulle.

'But the trial didn't go well,' Afam said. 'I flaked. The pressure was a lot. Making my family secure, paying back my friends and relatives. I couldn't get it out of my head, so I messed up the trial.'

'That's all well and good,' Annabel said. 'But how do you get from there to here? Why didn't you go home straight after?'

'I can't. Not until I've paid everyone back. I'm ashamed. Iman says not to worry, but it's embarrassing. I was screwed, and I made sure they screwed my neighbours as well. And anyway, they just completely dropped me, the club. They showed me the door and left me to make my own way back.'

'And you've never seen them again?'

At this, Afam seemed to change. His gaze flicked to the floor, 'No.' Sensing there was something more to this, Annabel pressed him.

'And what about back home — the guys who run the operation out of Nigeria?'

Afam winced this time. His breath caught. The decision to lie meant he took a fraction longer to answer.

'They don't want to know. I'm not important anymore. As far as they're concerned, they did their part. They took the money and ran. It happens all the time. There are guys here at the club who've been through a lot worse than I have. Ask Moussa. Sorry, I have to go.'

His last sentence was a full stop. Without hesitation, he stood up to leave.

'Look, Afam, sorry — I didn't mean to upset you. It must be hard thinking about your family back home. Here, take this.' Annabel passed him a card with her contact details. He glanced at it and stuffed it into the pocket of his tracksuit bottoms. 'It was great to meet you. I'll be in Paris for a few more days. If you want to talk more, just call. Any time.'

Once he had left the room, Annabel took out her phone and fired off a text to her editor.

Plot thickens. Going to stay for a few days. Can you cover for me?

The reply came after a few seconds.

Sure. Stay out of trouble.

2

The morning sun forced its way through the film of pollution that lingered on the Lagos skyline, obscuring the peaks of the tallest buildings on the skyline. The traders who lined the streets at the Boundary Market, just north of AJ City, didn't seem to notice as they clamoured for the attention of their next customers.

Afam deftly wound his way through the throng, pushing a shopping cart in front of him. He had already been working for hours, moving from pitch to pitch, filling his cart with plastic bottles and other recyclables, shuttling back and forth between the market and the recycling centre. For every kilogram of waste he picked up, he would collect points to put towards food, household items. Education. Iman was doing so well at school. He couldn't let her education be disrupted.

'Hey, Afam! How you dey?' Afam turned in the direction of the shout and saw his neighbour hanging from the rear of one of the yellow minibuses that filled the roads of the mega-city, rucksack slung over his shoulder, roller blades strapped to his feet.

'Stanley, I dey fine!' Afam smiled at the man, 'That helmet won't help much, eh?' Stanley took out one ear bud and let it dangle down from the collar of his t-shirt as he adjusted the neon green helmet, adorned with all manner of stickers and graffiti, on top of his braids, clipping the strap under his chin.

'Better?' Stanley cocked a grin on his face, twisting his head as though waiting for Afam to take a picture.

'Much. See you later?'

'You know it.'

Stanley pulled his scarf up over his mouth and nose and resumed his grip on the back of the minibus taxi as it pulled off, the traffic in front of it having cleared.

Afam continued along his route, picking up things to be recycled, separating the hard plastic lids from the bottles and placing them in his cart. The market was in full swing, with traders and shoppers shooting back and forth between stalls, negotiating the price of everything from fruit and vegetables to motor oil. He greeted everyone on his regular route. Some had even collected their waste for him and handed him a bag as he rolled past. He made a mental list of those people. He would pay them back for their small kindness one day.

His mind drifted into a daydream he must have had a million times over. Waiting in the tunnel at National Stadium, listening to the roar of the home fans waiting for the Nigerian national team to emerge onto the pitch. As he walked out of the tunnel, the noise increased, hitting him like a wave, and his heart swelled with pride.

He looked around, saw the flags waving, the scores of his countrymen creating a sea of green shirts. Out of the chaos, he heard the solitary wail of a single air horn. He couldn't focus on anything else.

The image in front of him dissolved. But the noise stayed, though broken now, switching from one long drone to short blasts. Afam tried to cling to the image of the stadium, tried to imagine singing the national anthem, but the horn slammed at the remaining fragments.

'Hey, fool, get out of the way!' Afam was back in the real world now, and turned to see two men on a scooter behind him. He had veered away from the path into the line of traffic. He darted back towards the pavement, careful not to topple his load of plastic. It was almost full anyway, so he turned and headed off to the recycling centre. He still had many hours to go before his friends got away from school.

* * *

The setting sun picked out a technicolour array from the haze over the Lagos sky. Deep pastel pinks and purples scalded into amber, ochre and the gleaming white of the star itself. Afam pulled on his jacket, zipping it up to his chin as he left the locker room and waved to the guys in the office. 'Same time tomorrow, Ayo.' Ayodele looked up from his computer momentarily, bringing his index finger to his forehead to give Afam a mock salute and a nod.

Leye was waiting for him outside, still in his school uniform, leather satchel slung over his shoulder. A pair of football boots that were older than he was dangled either side of his neck.

'You took your sweet time,' Leye said, already walking away down the road, forcing Afam to jog to catch up. 'They won't wait for us, and then we won't get on 'til half-time.'

'Relax, man. We'll get there — you might have to break a sweat, though,' Afam prodded his friend in his stomach as he overtook him, 'Think you can keep up?' He accelerated away and Leye gave chase, boots and bag clattering around him as he ran, looking like a pack mule that had darted from the caravan. He swung a wild leg at Afam's feet, but the other boy feinted away, hopping on the balls of his feet and landing without breaking his stride. Leye scooped up a bottle from the side of the road and flung it at Afam's back.

The boys ran on down the streets of AJ City. It was less busy than at the Boundary Market. The apartment buildings were smaller, more spread apart. There was less colour. The further you got from the centre of Lagos, the less vibrant things became. Gone were the heckles of street vendors, the thrum and smell of diesel engines, the music blaring from speakers and the seemingly endless rows of colourful fabrics and shop fronts. In their place stood ten-foot high walls made of drab concrete, addresses hastily daubed on corroded corrugated gates. People cared less about picking up the litter in these areas.

'Look, here he is, AJ's very own Okocha — hey, AJ Okocha!' The group assembled on the dusty patch of land that served as their home pitch all broke into laughter as Afam and Leye approached, making exaggerated prayer motions to the heavens. 'And look who's following him. Shittu!' At this, the teammates bellowed as one. Leye scowled.

'Just ignore them, Leye,' Afam consoled his friend as they both pulled on their trainers. Afam fingered the flap at the front where the sole was coming away from the leather.

The players split up into two teams and a game of scratch football began. This was no place for the soft tackles and fear of bookings that you found on professional pitches. Elbows were hurled as often as insults, shirts were not just pulled but torn and feet were left behind way too long in tackles.

As the game progressed, Leye and Afam's team fell behind, and the jeers grew louder. They always seemed to target Leye, and Afam could sense his friend getting more incensed with every insult.

'Leye, leave it, promise me?' Afam had seen his friend's temper get the better of him on more than one occasion, and didn't want to have to break up a fight.

The smaller kids and friends of the players were assembled on the sidelines and a cheer went up as Fatai, the ringleader who had been needling Leye all game, received the ball and set off at pace down the wing. Leye gave chase and was hot on Fatai's heels. He had almost caught him when Fatai released the ball into the box.

But Leye didn't care. He dived at Fatai with both feet, studs up and tore into his lower leg. The other boy crumpled to the floor, and the two tangled in a knot of limbs.

'You shouldn't let your mind wander, Fatai — it's too small to be let out on its own,' Leye smirked as he got up. Fatai snarled, his gaze shot like daggers at Leye.

'*Ode oshi!* You stupid fuck,' Fatai yelled, shoving Leye in his chest with both hands. Leye squared up to Fatai, the two boys butting their foreheads together. A group of men who'd been sitting back from the sidelines stood up and made their way to the altercation, their movements languid but determined. Having smelt blood, the wolves were circling.

Afam, watching closely, made his way over to Leye and placed a hand on his friend's shoulder. 'Leye, come, leave this.' Out of the corner of his eye, he saw the group of men push their way through the supporters who had gathered around the two boys. 'Seriously, Leye, come.' He put his arm around Leye's chest and pulled his friend away.

'That's right, pussy, back away,' Fatai spat the words and Afam had to tighten his grip around his friend. 'Look,' he said, trying to distract Leye, 'It's Iman — don't let her see you like this.'

Afam waved to his sister, who had sat on an overturned crate at the far end of the pitch and was reading her book. Leye looked up, and Afam felt him relax.

'Hey, Immy!' Leye called out to her, 'Always reading... School's over — can't you enjoy the sunshine?'

* * *

Afam and Leye flanked Iman as they walked home, the two boys kicking a plastic bottle between them, plumes of dust puffing from the road as they scuffed the ground.

'Have you heard from your cousin?' Iman asked Leye.

'No one has. I think he must be so busy he hasn't had the chance yet.'

'Must be a lot going on. Where was his trial?' There was scepticism in Iman's voice.

'Dortmund,' Leye announced with pride, 'I'm telling you, it won't be long before we see AJ City represented in the Champions League!' He didn't notice the subtle shake of her head, the roll of her eyes. The fate of the young Nigerians who were taken from their homes on false pretences of football stardom was an open secret amongst the locals. There were some semi-legitimate organisations who had links to European clubs, but the number of spots they could offer was tiny. Some lads who went out there came back with their hopes shattered. Worst were the ones who stayed; some by choice, others through shame. What was more insidious, though, were the gangs who would scout the makeshift pitches around the cities and approach kids, promising them trials at European clubs that never existed. Villages would raise thousands of dollars and hand it over to these Area Boys to cover 'expenses' to send the young men away — piling not only all of their money, but all of their hope into these false promises. But then the 'managers' disappeared, leaving people stranded in another country that they had been smuggled into, with no money, no documentation, no shelter, nothing. Iman didn't like to think about what those boys had to do to survive so far away from home.

A vehicle moved past them slowly from behind and as it overtook, Afam saw the insignia of a local evangelical missionary church: 'Preach the Word' emblazoned on the side of the white fifteen-seater minibus. The brake lights engaged, and the van pulled up just ahead. Afam and Leye shared a glance, Afam's brow creasing into a frown. Neither of them knew anyone from Preach the Word. It wasn't in their neighbourhood.

The van came to a stop and the driver's door opened. The driver emerged, dressed in the standard issue Christian missionary outfit.

In his mid-thirties, he wore a crystal white polo shirt, buttoned up to the top, that he had tucked the shirt into a pair of grey-beige cargo shorts. His calf-length tube socks were pulled high and his New Balance trainers looked fresh out of the box.

The man waved at the approaching trio, a smile spreading from ear to ear. Though, Iman noticed, it didn't seem to reach his eyes.

'Hi, guys, how are you?' he swept back a blonde forelock and adjusted his wire-framed spectacles.

'Fine, thank you. Have a nice day.' It was Leye who answered, trying to shut down the conversation before it had started.

'You know, I saw you guys playing back there. I thought you had some genuine talent,' the man persisted. 'I'm Samuel, by the way. Sam.'

'Nice to meet you, Sam,' Afam spoke up. The two boys had unconsciously moved closer to Iman. 'We have to get home. I need to help with dinner and Iman needs to study.'

'Iman, that's a beautiful name! And who are you guys? You must be her brother, right?' Afam, Leye and Iman had walked past where he had parked his van, which meant that he was following them now, though maintaining a respectful distance. 'Okay, I get it. You guys are busy — I don't want to hold you up. I just wanted to give you a gift...'

Afam turned to Sam, who held his hands outstretched, a pair of brand-new Adidas Copa Mundial boots.

'I figured you were about a size nine? These were donated by a family back where I'm from in Michigan. Given how I just saw you playing back there, I can't think of a much better home for them.'

Afam turned back to his sister and Leye, raising his eyebrows in question. Leye shrugged, pouting his lower lip. It felt bad to take the gift; he would never go to the man's church. But opportunities like this didn't come very often. He opened his rucksack and placed the boots inside.

'Thank you, Sam — I'll pay you back.'

'No, no. No need for that, they're a gift. God blessed you with your skills, it's the least I can do to help you perform at your best, showing the beauty of His divine glory.' Sam was smiling again, this time seemingly with his whole being, as though he were directly communing with God.

Afam gave his thanks again and turned back to Iman and Leye.

'See you around!' Sam called after them as they turned their backs and headed back along the road towards home.

'Iman, promise me you won't mention this to mom,' Afam said to his sister. He feared that if his mother found out that he had a brand new pair of boots, she would make him take them to Boundary Market and sell them. They needed money. His dreams would have to wait.

3

The weather had turned. The beauty of Paris was no longer picked out by glorious sunshine, and Annabel now had to suffer the city in the rain. Despite the romanticism that surrounded the city, which she herself fell victim to, she had always marvelled at how dirty it was. Hidden amongst the stone facades and wrought-iron balconies were layers of grit and grime, accentuated by the twilight served by the grey skies overhead.

It seemed like homelessness had risen astronomically since she'd last visited. A story that had run in her paper had estimated that whilst homelessness and the problems associated with inadequate housing were on the rise across the country, in Paris it had risen by around eighty-four per cent. Like every other city in the developed world, wages had stagnated whilst private rents had risen, forcing people into squalor. For many, having a job was no longer a guarantee of housing security. Historical under-investment in affordable housing development only exacerbated the problem. People couldn't afford to buy, so they had to rent. Landlords kept raising the rent to fit the market. It was capitalism run riot. Parisians seemed sympathetic to the homeless, more so than Annabel had witnessed in London, but only if it wasn't on their doorstep. Residents in the city's most affluent quarter — the sixteenth *arrondissement* — had rebelled against plans to build a homeless shelter in their neighbourhood. Not in my backyard, seemed to be the attitude from the people who actually had the money and influence to make a difference.

Annabel could feel the low pressure and retrieved an umbrella from her bag, anticipating rain. A born and bred Londoner, she was no stranger to rain, but heavy showers sprang up on you in Paris. The heavens opened, drenching everything below. At least it washed away some of the filth, Annabel thought. The pavement took on the sheen of the streetlights and storefronts as she walked past, blurring the edges of everything into a live-action Impressionist rendering of the city.

A few more blocks and she had reached the building where she was due to meet her contact. Moussa had given Annabel Éloïse's contact details and after a brief exchange of emails, they had set a meeting. Éloïse worked for an NGO set up to end human trafficking, and her work was specifically geared towards tracing and helping those people who had been trafficked out of the African continent. There were many people who came to France from the old colonial territories, in what had been known then as French West Africa. For decades, almost none of the Africans living in those colonies were considered citizens. They had been 'subjects', stripped of rights before the law, the rights to property ownership, to travel, to vote. To dissent. Whilst independence had been gained in many cases, the legacy of colonialism lived on. Many Africans were forced to leave their homelands to seek better things for themselves and their families. The irony, of course, was that the country which had once ruled them now turned its back on them and so alternative means of migration became necessary. There was little change of stopping immigration, but like anything, driving it underground only empowered the criminal gangs, who were more than happy to part people with their cash on the promise of a better life.

Annabel cast her eye over the buzzer and pressed the button for *Humains Sans Frontières* and waited for a response. Moments later, a buzzer barked into the street, adding to the cacophony of Parisian life, accompanied by the heavy clunk of the door unlocking. Annabel took hold of the brass doorknob set in the middle of a heavy oak door and pushed. The door closed behind her, blocking out the clamour that had assaulted her on the street. She placed her umbrella, still thankfully dry, in the bucket by the door and began climbing the twisting marble staircase.

As she reached the *palier* at the top of the first flight of steps, a smart young woman, dressed head to toe in chic black office casual, was there to meet her. Annabel felt as though she was about to enter the offices of French Vogue and felt distinctly under-dressed. Given that she'd not been planning to stay more than one night, she'd packed light and had been wearing the same outfit three days in a row now.

'Annabel?' the young woman asked, raising an inquisitive eyebrow.

'Hi,' Annabel said, holding out a hand, 'Éloïse?'

'*Oui!*' Éloïse said, a warm smile spreading across her face, 'Hi! So great to meet you.' She ignored Annabel's proffered hand and took her by the shoulders, pulling her in and planting a kiss in the air on either side of Annabel's face. No matter how embedded she became amongst London's media elite, Annabel had never quite got used to the trend towards kissing and hugging to greet someone. Especially someone you'd just met. The pandemic had been bliss for her as people hadn't wanted to get too close to others. Clearly this hadn't extended to France. She returned Éloïse's smile, but after a few nights of poor sleep on a mattress that seemed older than she was, couldn't quite match her energy and enthusiasm.

'And you,' Annabel said. 'Sorry I'm a bit late, but I've been running around town all morning. You lose a minute here a minute there and eventually it all catches up to you.'

'Don't worry about it,' Éloïse replied, swiping a hand in the space between them to dismiss Annabel's concerns, 'You're on Paris time. Everyone's always ten minutes late for everything.'

'Like London time,' Annabel said. 'I think it's just city time, isn't it?'

'You've clearly never been to Geneva... those guys make Germans look relaxed about punctuality. Anyway, let's not stand out here in the cold all day — come in. Can I get you something to drink?'

'Coffee would be great, thanks,' Annabel said as she was ushered into Éloïse's office. The office reminded Annabel of a newsroom. Desks were dotted around seemingly at random, space made ad hoc as teams grew and shrank in line with funding. Each desk was littered with an assortment of papers and coffee mugs, cigarette packets and vape pens. Whilst the rest of Western Europe was moving towards a complete ban on smoking in public places, the act still had a certain *je ne sais quoi* in France.

The workstation that bucked the trend was the reception desk, which was spotless, mirroring the pristine middle-aged gentleman who manned it. The phone headset wrapped around his head seemed incapable of putting a hair out of place in his immaculately manicured coiffure. He tapped at his workstation, which emitted the pleasant click-clack of an old-school mechanical keyboard, raising his head as Éloïse and Annabel walked past to deliver a small nod of acknowledgement, a brief, hospitable smile before turning his attention back to his work.

Éloïse took Annabel through to a small partitioned room in the back corner. She drew the Venetian blinds that obscured the floor-to-ceiling windows that formed one wall of the office and left to fetch drinks. Whilst she was gone, Annabel dug around in her bag for the tools of her trade, fetching out her Dictaphone and notepad and placing them on the white plastic veneer IKEA table ubiquitous in offices across the globe.

A few minutes later, Éloïse returned with a cafetiere of coffee and two mugs, which she placed on the table next to them as she took her seat.

'So,' Annabel started, as Éloïse poured the drinks, 'First of all, thanks so much for meeting me on such short notice.'

'Not a problem,' Éloïse said, sipping from her mug, 'Always happy to spread the word. We need all the exposure we can get. Funding isn't what it used to be. Charity is the first thing to go when people have to cut back. It's not helped at all, of course, by the sort of extreme right-wing sentiment we're seeing emerge in France right now. When your world goes to shit, circle the wagons, stop helping others, blame everyone else, think only of yourself...'

'Completely,' Annabel agreed. 'So how does that play into what you do? Of course, people are less able to put their hand in their pocket, but you have other sources of funding, big money donors. But do you think there's been a change in attitude towards what you do?'

'Straight to business! That was smooth. I'm impressed.' Éloïse smiled, 'I don't know. I'm not sure people are thinking 'well, fuck those other guys' in a really pointed way. They're just too focused on their own stuff. They're worrying if they'll be able to feed their kids, not whether someone else can feed theirs. That sort of thing extends to what we do, sure. As long as people are worried about being able to keep the heating on, they're going to find it easy to hate the people who are 'stealing their jobs' — and that's what the furthest fringes of the right wing are convincing them is happening. And from there, sure, people stop caring so much about the plight of immigrants and asylum seekers. The powers that be use them as scapegoats to fuel anti-immigration agendas and then we lose the support of powerful people in government — it's not a 'good look',' she made air quotes with her fingers, 'To be helping immigrants when naturalised citizens are starving at home.'

'It's like Brexit,' Annabel offered. 'People voted to take back control, but equally people had been told that 'foreigners' were coming to the UK and taking up all the good jobs. Now look — all the foreigners are gone, all the jobs are open, but no one wants them.'

'Exactly. Exactly that. Except in our case it's not Romanian fruit pickers, it's Africans leaving war-torn countries to come and clean our toilets. It's big business, trafficking. Nearly $150 billion a year. Forty million people trapped in conditions of modern slavery worldwide according to the global slavery index. That's a lot of people. You can't ignore that many people. But people do. Everyone does. We let these people clean our kitchens, scrub our floors, do all manner of things, and we don't stop to think about how they got here. Why they came here. They get given the invisible jobs. Out of sight, out of mind.'

'So, listen, you know I came here with some pretty specific questions, right?' Annabel interrupted Éloïse before she could get her pitch off the ground. It was clear Éloïse was passionate about her work, genuinely moved by the plight of the people she sought to help, but Annabel needed to keep her on track, not get caught up in a sales pitch about the value of the work Éloïse and her team were doing. She needed to get things moving on her story.

'Moussa told me you could shed some light on the trafficking of boys — I think it seems to be mainly boys — out of Africa on the false promise of football trials? He seemed to suggest it was a growing problem, that traffickers were taking everything these kids had, smuggling them through the continent and over the sea in perilous conditions, and then either abandoning them, or forcing them into a sort of indentured servitude, stealing their money, their passports. Taking a cut out of the payslips of some, but forcing others into working for the gangs, turning to lives of criminality.'

'Oh, for sure,' Éloïse confirmed Moussa's speculations, 'It's a pretty huge part of the problem. Each year, about twenty-thousand kids at least are trafficked out of Africa into Europe to "play football." Of course, of those twenty-thousand not many are legit. People pretending to be football agents create bogus interest from foreign clubs. They go to these families and they offer them a chance for a better life.

In Cameroon, the average salary of a footballer is $100 a month. If one of their kids could make it, even at a lower league club, they could support the whole family. It's hard to imagine how poor some of these people are. Of course we have poverty everywhere, and it's getting worse, but the situation in somewhere like Cameroon is like nothing you will ever know.

So, of course, these parents do everything they can to create the opportunity for their kids. Sometimes they're convinced to hand over significant amounts of money, that they scrape together from everyone they know, in order to send their kids off. But it's just exploitation. These fake agents take money from the family to cover costs, and then when the player gets to the destination country, they're abandoned, usually after their passport and money has been taken from them.

They end up staying in the country illegally through a mix of circumstance and shame, with no way of making money. This, of course, leads them to head underground. From there it doesn't take long for criminals to get their claws into them, and they're forced into all manner of things: forced labour, sexual exploitation, domestic servitude, debt bondage...

I heard about one case from a colleague who handles Cameroon, a player got on a flight from Douala to Doha, his family had paid $10,000 to the agent who arranged the flight, but there was no one waiting for him in Doha. He didn't even make it out of the airport. They jailed a Cameroon politician for that one, a small win.

On the other side of the coin, in 2007, they found a boat washed up on the shore of Tenerife. One-hundred-and-thirty young African men were on board, fifteen of whom thought they were going for trials at Real Madrid and Marseille. We might be winning battles, but we're losing the war.'

'I remember that story,' Annabel said. 'I read the prosecutor's report. It said something like forty per cent of all Cameroonian transfers were some sort of scam.'

'That doesn't surprise me. It's not just the obvious illegal gangs who are trafficking people. Unfortunately, football in Africa is not about winning matches or titles. It is about finding the next big star to sell... even through the legitimate channels, these kids and their families end up being exploited.

They're lured into unfair practices, treated as commodities with no rights, whose value depends on their capacity to work and from which they expect to make a profit. They auction these kids off to sports franchises and clubs around the world, in a quest to maximise the financial return on their investment. It's child slavery on an international scale.

In most cases, clubs aren't even doing much to hide it: Chelsea, Real Madrid, Barca — they've all had transfer bans recently for violating FIFA rules on international transfers of minors. In some cases, these clubs are arranging the adoptions of players by European families to skirt the rules. Imagine what's happening at the lower levels. There's no regulation. No repercussions.

There are hundreds of unlicensed academies all over Africa. Look at Ghana. When Michael Essien signed for Chelsea at £70,000 a week, his story became one of hope for kids all over the country. But overnight, hundreds of academies popped up, thousands of 'agents'. Sometimes they do get players onto the books of a lower league club, but they take the lion's share of the kids salary to pay back their investment. They dole out pocket money to the players, to keep them dependent on the agents, and then the agent vanishes when it comes to the end of that first year contract. I'll give you two guesses what happens to lots of those kids. They get dropped, their visas run out... you know the rest.'

'So how does it stop? What can you do?'

'The solution to human trafficking is not one size fits all. Football trafficking is a subset of the wider issue of human trafficking, and there's a lack of understanding from the public and the policy-makers about the unique incentives that football provides to both the perpetrators and potential victims of this crime. It's an international problem, it's not just France. You saw the news about the Italian club being given a two-year transfer ban for breaching rules governing the international transfer of minors. They illegally brought in thirteen underage Nigerian players over four years. FIFA calls it "breaching rules", we call it "football trafficking." Like with any form of international collaboration, it's next to impossible to get everyone to align.

We need key organisations to make an effort to balance the opportunities given to those from developing and developed countries. We need more transparency for aspiring athletes coming from developing countries. When they can see that there is a 'legal route' to success in Europe, they will be less likely to depend on unscrupulous persons to make their dreams come true.

'What about the UK? Is anything happening there?' Annabel asked. The problem seemed insurmountable, and so far they were only talking about football trafficking.

Éloïse sighed. 'Yes, and no. We have a team we collaborate with in the UK, but it's hard for them to make any headway as it's a lot of the time it's tied up with the private school system and those guys, with their old boys' network, are basically untouchable. They get round the FIFA regulations so easily. They ship in players under sixteen to these private schools, with their immigration documents saying they're moving to be educated. Their costs are covered by agents and club officials then they link up with football teams when they're in the country. Or, being less deceitful, they just bring under-eighteens to play only in friendlies. They secure the player, then register them on their eighteenth birthday.'

'But what's in it for the agents? They can't be making any money out of these non-transfers?'

'Pfft, that's easy,' Éloïse smiled, 'The agents invoice for 'scouting services' — there's no age limit on that.'

'Okay, going back slightly — that's a lot of people to not get noticed. Why isn't the government paying more attention?' Annabel asked.

'I think some parts of government are. But we're talking about a major operation here. It's not just the fake actors pretending to be agents and intermediaries between academies and clubs, there are people at powerful sports bodies, at foreign embassies, who are turning a blind eye to it. Obviously, they're on the payroll, but it's hard enough to trace the kids, let alone the people who brought them here.

There's silence from the kids when we do find them; they're too scared to speak out for fear of reprisals. Not just for them, but for their families back home. And anyway, going after the traffickers is only half the battle. We all know what happens when you cut off the head of the Hydra. To really stop this in its tracks, we need to go after those at the top — not the heads of the gangs, but the people who enable them to do what they do.'

'What's in it for these government organisations, though?' Annabel asked. Part of her position as journalist was to keep asking questions, to strip the hearsay out of everything and keep digging until she got to the root, 'Individual kickbacks, that's easy — border guards who don't look too closely at documents, back-office staff who rubber-stamp sketchy visa applications. But you're suggesting that the government knows about this stuff and is letting it carry on. Why? As you say, they want to skirt around rising anti-immigrant feeling that's spreading across Europe, so why facilitate more illegal immigration? Money is one thing, but it's not a "good look"...'

'There's a lot of money changing hands. In fact, I want to put you in touch with someone who's working inside one of these organisations. So far, there's very little data to support our claims. Only a few studies have been conducted on sports trafficking, so there is a lack of quantitative and verifiable data and actual research on this topic is based largely on media reports. Chloé, however, says she's got her hands on some pretty explosive stuff. She wants to go public with it. I told her I'd pass over her details to you. I hope you don't mind?'

'Not at all,' Annabel said, sensing the meeting was coming to an end. 'Just whip it over in an email.' Annabel started packing her things into her bag. 'Thanks again for meeting me on short notice. And thanks for the coffee.'

'Sure thing. Good luck with your story. Here, I'll show you out.'

'Oh, it's okay, don't worry — I think I remember,' Annabel said.

'Hey, if you're ever at a loose end, or need to go over a few things, let me know. I live in the city. We can hook up.'

Annabel was taken aback. 'Thanks,' she said politely. 'I'll make sure to do that.' She smiled, and instantly regretted it. She didn't want to appear though she were reciprocating the flirtation.

Éloïse gave a knowing smile, her confidence not so much as dented, as she stood and held out a hand. Annabel flushed red as she shook the other woman's hand and made for the exit.

4

Afam's head hung low as he made his way to the pitch. It had not been a good day. He hadn't collected many credits. There wouldn't be enough for Iman's school credits and their usual amount of groceries. He could feel his stomach cramping, anticipating the hunger.

His feet dragged as he walked down the road, the sound of the scraping gravel masking the sound of the car coming up from behind him. He turned and saw the same van that had pulled up beside them yesterday. Samuel, his floppy blonde hair tucked under a cotton baseball cap, gave a friendly blast on the horn. The van was approaching at pace, and Afam made himself small so that it could pass, but it van slowed as it pulled up next to him.

'Need a lift?' Afam turned and saw Samuel beaming at him through the wound-down window.

It had been a long day and though he desperately wanted to give his new boots a try, the prospect of the walk to the pitches was an unwelcome one. 'Sure,' he said.

The door clunked open and Afam hauled his bag inside before climbing into the front passenger seat. It seemed strange to sit in the back when there was no one else with them.

'I take it you're heading back over to the pitches from the other day?' Sam asked him as he put the vehicle in gear and pulled off again.

'It's not too far out of your way, is it?' Afam asked. 'You could take me as far as the school and I can walk from there.'

'No, it's fine,' said Sam. 'I remember the way. What are friends for?'

They drove a while in silence, Afam watching out the window at the streets rolling by. On one side of the street, weather-beaten corrugated sheet metal spread haphazardly across the top of crumbling cement blocks to form the places he and his neighbours called home. Across the road sat a new building, the red brick popping against the drab grey sky behind. The local kids called this place Castle Dracula. A round tower sat on one side of the building. Arched window openings traced the route of the staircase to the upper floor, though the top floor windows had the shades permanently drawn. People had invented elaborate folklore about what exactly went on up there, in the dead of night. It was unlikely any of them would ever find out. The house was closed off to the street by steel gates several inches thick, the filigree metalwork doing little to distract from the iron spikes and barbed wire that traced the boundary wall. Afam's eye was drawn by lush palm trees behind the walls, stretching into the sky and fanning out their leaves like fireworks.

'Hey, are you okay? You seem quiet?' Sam broke the silence, his last sentence coming out as a question.

Afam sighed, took a moment to answer.

'I'm fine. Today was a hard day,' he said, and then, 'Thank you for asking.'

Afam could feel himself warming to Sam. Like all the other kids in the neighbourhood, he had always been wary of the 'white saviours' who came to the neighbourhoods to help 'savages' like themselves find God, but Sam seemed like a decent guy, didn't seem pushy with his faith. So far.

'So... you go to school near here?' Sam continued making polite conversation and Afam began to open up to him. Told him how he'd dropped out of school to help his mother, and his job collecting waste to convert into tuition fees for Iman.

'We couldn't afford to send both of us to school, and she's the one to back. I never really got on at school. No point throwing good money after bad.'

'Hey,' Sam adopted a conciliatory tone, 'We each have our own set of talents. Iman's great at books, but I bet she can't run rings around those other boys like I saw you do the other day.'

That got a smile out of Afam. 'Actually, she's pretty good at football. There's not a lot she isn't good at... but I take your point.' He grabbed his bag from the seat in between them. 'It's just up here, Sam. You can drop me off here.'

Sam indicated, letting other drivers know there was a foreigner in the car, and pulled over. Afam pushed open the door and hopped out, making his way across the dusty field.

'I'll see you around,' Sam called out after him. 'Hope those boots give you an extra boost. You can show up that guy from yesterday.'

Afam turned, boots in hand, and raised them aloft, 'See you!' And with that, he turned and ran to where the others were already playing.

* * *

The game had lifted Afam's spirits some way, and he and Leye joked and laughed as they made their way home. The sun had dipped below the horizon. There were no streetlights in Ajegunle but, as the boys made their way from the football field, they were guided by the halogen lamps of the street food vendors, bars and brothels that dotted the city streets.

Groups of men sat outside beer parlours on plastic garden furniture, crowded around TV screens showing football, shouting obscenities above the racket of the generators that combated the prolonged power outages they were used to in this part of the city. The smell of diesel mingled with the barbecue smell of the spiced meat being cooked on grills along the path.

'Oh man, I'm hungry. This place has the best *suya* in Lagos,' Leye said.

Afam rolled his eyes.

'Does he pay you to say this? You know it's me, Leye, you don't have to give me the marketing speak? I got some tips today, anyway — let's get some food.'

The two boys approached the stall where a man worked, turning skewered meat over a makeshift grill that comprised a rusty oil barrel cut in half down its length with a section of wire mesh placed on top. As he turned the meat, the fat dripped off onto the pile of coals in the drum, delicate sizzles giving birth to small licks of flame which spat up and embraced the food, coating it with layers of smoky char. Afam was salivating as he and Leye ordered a portion each before taking a seat on a nearby wall to watch the world go by.

It was the weekend, and the city was in full swing. Ajegunle was a very poor part of the city and the residents worked hard to make ends meet most of the time, which meant that come the end of the week, they often had a lot of steam to blow off. There weren't many cars, the packed streets made it difficult to navigate. The banana yellow minibuses you found in the city were replaced by tuk-tuks — or *keke* as they were called locally -- and mopeds and scooters darted around, revving their engines hard as they nipped in and out of the crowds. Afam watched as one motorbike cut in and out of the crowd, passing deliberately, dangerously close to pedestrians. Neither the driver nor the passenger — gripping white-knuckled to the back of the bike — wore a helmet so Afam could see the vicious grins on their faces as they witnessed the havoc they were causing.

'These Area Boys, man,' Leye shook his head, 'What do they think they're doing? These are their people...'

'It's bad, I know... but what can you do? There's nothing to do here. No jobs, no money... we can't all be such upstanding members of society like you, Leye,' Afam jabbed his friend in the arm.

'Bullshit. You can't blame everything on the government. Sure, they're as big a set of crooks as the purse-snatchers and drug dealers, but there are a million ways to find work. Even if there was work, you think those guys would take it? They think the world owes them something — they just take, take, take. Why find honest work when you can take what someone else has worked hard to earn?'

'Okay, man...' Afam saw little point in having the same conversation again. 'Hey, isn't that your cousin?'

Leye looked up sharply from his *suya.* He wiped the spicy grease from his mouth with the back of his hand, and his eyes narrowed as another scooter whizzed past. Sure enough, as they sped past, he could make out his cousin's dreadlocks tied up in a pineapple on top of his head, the lower portion of his skull shaved close in an undercut.

Leye sighed so heavily that it seemed like his whole body had deflated. His eyes rolled back, and he stared up at the sky, slowly shaking his head, muttering barely audible curses. He puffed his cheeks and blew out through his mouth as he dragged himself back to look down the street as his cousin and his friends continued to dodge and weave through the crowds.

'Hey, moron!' Leye shouted as the scooter carrying his cousin drew near. His cousin's head snapped round, violence in his bloodshot eyes. He smirked as he realised who it was and tapped the driver on the shoulder. The scooter trundled towards Afam and Leye and the boy on the back hopped off before it had come to a standstill.

'Leye, cuz, how na?' Leye's cousin held out a fist, a greeting that Leye pointedly refused to reciprocate. His cousin smiled and shrugged his shoulders. 'How's it going, Afam — still going to play for the Super Eagles?'

'Hey, Semi. Yeah, something like that.' Afam had always got on with Leye's cousin. They'd played together as kids, but recently, Semi had started hanging around with a rough crowd. Afam was sure Semi was just keeping himself occupied, but his new friends were involved in all sorts of criminality and racketeering. Given the state he seemed to be in, Afam didn't bet on it being too long before Semi got involved with more than just Friday night joyrides.

'See, Moses,' Semi turned to the man driving the scooter, 'This is the guy I was telling you about. The next big thing out of AJ City!'

The driver of the moped looked Afam up and down.

'I can make you a big star, my friend,' Moses said.

'Yeah, sure.' Afam had heard it all before.

'No, no, it's the truth, man. I know someone in the city who has a contact in Paris. A man from near here,' Moses planted a hand on Afam's shoulder. Countless dents and scars traced his knuckles, telling the story of the life that Moses had lived on the streets of Lagos. A white line ran through the meaty part of his thumb as though someone had tried to cleave it off. Or perhaps he'd fended off a machete blow — one of the favoured weapons of the gangs around here. 'Just get the money together for your travel and expenses. Before long, you'll be sipping champagne with Mbappé, as long as you get it right at your trial.'

'Sure, sure,' Afam was in no mood to argue. It was almost cliche, this story. The gangs made big promises about contacts in Europe and trials at huge clubs, and the unlucky, hopeful kids would gather as much as they could. They would get to Europe, that much was true. But when they arrived, they were stranded — no contact, no trial, no riches. No ride home. Even if they could afford it, most would be too embarrassed to return home, and so they got caught up in the system, working menial jobs and living in hovels thousands of miles from home. Sometimes you heard of someone making it, of the trial being real, but all that really did was create more false hope for the gangs to prey on.

Leye and his cousin made small talk for a while, then a piercing scream went up from the end of the street. There was a commotion as a fight broke out between a group of men and one of the kids on scooters.

'Come,' Moses tipped his head towards the racket and Semi jumped on the back of the moped.

'See you later, boys,' Semi shouted as he and Moses sped off towards the fight. Afam doubted they were on their way to mediate.

'Come on,' Leye said, tossing the container that had held his suya onto the ground. 'Let's get out of here.'

Afam looked around for a bin in which to place his litter. Finding nothing, he dropped it where he sat and stood up from the wall.

'Don't listen to Moses, Afam,' Leye sensed his friend daydreaming again. 'They're crooks. They can't give you anything except a headache.'

5

Afam waved at Sam, who was waiting by his car. Sam had started hanging around at the football field a lot more and occasionally he had offered the boys and Iman a ride home. Leye held back as Afam made his way across to his new friend.

'Come on, Leye — I can't be bothered to walk today,' Afam said, breaking into a light jog to meet his new friend.

'Hey, Afam. You looked great out there. The new boots seem to be treating you well?' Sam gave Afam a brief hug, and the two turned to Leye, Sam resting his arm along Afam's shoulders. 'Hey, Leye — long time no see, eh?'

Leye did not return Sam's greeting, and Afam noticed him clenching his teeth. He moved away from Sam and took his friend around the shoulders. He could feel the tension carrying through Leye's whole body. Did he feel threatened by Afam's new friendship?

'Are you okay?' Afam brought his head close to Leye's.

'I'm fine,' Leye struggled out of Afam's embrace, 'It's a beautiful day, I don't want a ride. Walk with me?'

'I've been working all day, Leye, and that game was tough — that new kid at the back had a lot of pace, don't you think? I'm going to go with Sam,' Afam was already backing away from Leye towards the open car door, 'I'll see you tomorrow?' But Leye had turned his back.

'What's up with him?' Sam said as Afam closed the door to the minibus. He slung his bag in the footwell and leaned back against the window, putting his feet up on the seats.

'Who knows? He gets like this sometimes. I've not seen him for days. Moody guy, you know?'

Sam smiled a knowing smile. 'I've known a few of those in my time! Anyway, I'm kind of glad he's not here. I have something I want to talk to you about. I don't want Leye getting jealous.' He started the engine and pulled away down the dirt track. They spoke for a while about nothing in particular. Afam was complaining about the influx of companies being set up to clear the streets of Lagos.

'They give people fancy uniforms, bikes, vans — I can't compete with that! It takes me half a day to collect what they can in an hour.'

'I guess some would call that progress...'

'Seems to me like progress just means fewer people make more money. Where does that leave the rest of us?'

Sam didn't know what to say to that, so just carried on driving, his eyes fixed to the road ahead.

'Hey, where are we going? I need to get home,' Afam hadn't been paying attention, but he vaguely recognised where they were as somewhere in Satellite Town.

'Remember I said that I needed to talk to you about something? I just wanted to take us somewhere we could be sure we weren't overheard, or seen. Like I said, I don't want Leye getting upset and you know better than I do how rumours spread through this place.' Sam noticed Afam's hesitancy, 'Relax, it's something good. I can guarantee you'll like what I have to say.'

Sam pulled the van off of the road and they parked up by the water. The southern part of the city was awash with creeks and inlets that branched off from Lagos Lagoon and the Gulf of Guinea. Channels had been carved from the natural waterways, redirecting water to some of the properties on the waterfront, forming moats around the concrete foundations. Scaffold boards were laid across the water to provide access. Afam baulked as he noticed PVC waste pipes feeding directly into the moat at one house. It was as good a deterrent as any, he supposed.

'So, what is this secret information you have, Sam?' Afam raised his eyebrows, teasing the preacher.

'Well, it's good news for you,' Sam began, 'You know that I work here as a missionary of course... no, no, don't worry, I respect that you have your own faith. This isn't about that.' Sam unclipped his seatbelt and turned to Afam. 'Well, we have missions set up all around Lagos, all around Nigeria. Around Africa, actually. And part of our mission is to link up with local businesses and provide opportunity for local kids, supported by the church.'

Afam stayed silent, nodding as he listened to Sam. Despite what Sam had said, he could feel some preaching coming up.

'Well, one of my colleagues — a friend, actually, we went to high school together back home — works in Port Harcourt. One of his outreach schemes runs in conjunction with the Rivers United youth squad. I got chatting to him about you and... well, he's pulled some strings and Rivers have agreed for you to visit them for a tryout.'

Afam couldn't quite believe what he was hearing. Of course he had heard similar from the scammers like Moses, but coming from Sam the offer seemed to be genuine. He felt light-headed, his mind started racing. He could barely contain his excitement.

'Sam! What? Are you serious?'

Sam nodded, smiling at Afam, 'Totally serious. So, should I tell him yes? We can sort out the logistics of getting you there once we have a date. I can cover your expenses for the travel through the mission and make sure your mom gets some money so you don't miss out on the tokens you'd have got from your collections.'

'You're serious? Really?' Afam asked again, it felt too good to be true. But Sam was a good man, a Christian man. He loved to give. He'd given him the boots, hadn't he? Afam leapt forward and wrapped his arms around Sam in a bear hug. 'I owe you, man, big time!'

Sam returned the hug, wrapping his arms around Afam bringing one hand up to the back of his head and pulling him close. Afam drew back but felt Sam pull him close again. He pushed back harder and Sam released his grasp.

'So... what next? Do I need to do anything?' Afam asked, straightening his t-shirt, confusion etched on his face.

'No, nothing — I'll be in touch with Gerry and organise the finer details,' Sam said. Afam noticed a change in him. There was a strange sneer on his face, a hunger in his eyes. 'Well, there is one thing... new boots, a trial at Rivers United... it seems like I'm doing a lot for you, friend, but what am I getting in return?'

'Anything,' Afam blurted, 'Just name it.'

'I'm so glad you said that,' Sam said, and he closed the gap between them. His hand moved to Afam's thigh and Afam felt him squeeze. It sent a shiver of revulsion through him but he felt frozen to the spot, his brain stuck between fight and flight mode, like a deer in headlights. 'There's only one thing I need.' Afam noticed Sam's other hand was rubbing at the crotch of his own pants.

Afam felt Sam's hand move further up his leg, moving beneath the fabric of his shorts and the sensation snapped him out of his trance. He pushed Sam hard, and the man fell back against the driver's side window.

'What the fuck are you doing?' he yelled, reaching into the foot well to grab his bag. Sam threw out his hand and grabbed the other end, using it to pull Afam close again.

'If you can't pay for those boots, Afam, I can find someone who will,' Afam shuddered again at the change in the man who until moments ago he had considered a friend. He hit at Sam's hand and pushed him again, scrambling around behind him for the door handle. The lock clunked and Afam spilled out onto the dirt. As Sam made his way across the seats, Afam slammed the door back into his face and turned and ran. He didn't stop running until he found the expressway. After catching his breath, he headed in the opposite direction of the setting sun. It would be a long walk home.

6

Almost before Annabel had left Éloïse's offices, an email notification had pinged through on her phone. It contained links to several news stories, government white papers and other official documents. It also contained the contact details of Chloé Martin. Annabel had to wait several days, and suffer through a handful of last-minute rearrangements, but had eventually managed to pin Chloé down. They had agreed to meet in a park near where Chloé lived, before she went to work.

Annabel had arrived early. She always had trouble sleeping in hotel rooms. Something about not being surrounded by her home comforts meant she always felt on edge. She always seemed to wake up at the crack of dawn, some noise from housekeeping or other guests leaving jolting her out of half-sleep. Nothing she did ever enabled her to fall back to sleep. So she had packed her bag for the day, slipped on her comfortable running shoes and walked across town to the meeting point.

It took an hour or so for Annabel to reach the Parc Monceau, and she had enjoyed the chance to witness the twilight time when the night shift and the day shift cross over. Security guards, night porters, nurses all finishing their day, making their way home. The subtle incongruity of dinners being eaten in the morning. Annabel had once known a man who'd worked night shifts. He was occasionally found in the pub by his train station, a few pints deep, at breakfast time. In contrast, the park wardens, bakers and street sweepers were just getting started. And the younger crowd who still hadn't gone to bed, wide-eyed, pupils dilated, grey-skinned, hoodies thrown over crumpled couture outfits, trying to drum up the courage to eat something before they crashed out.

Annabel entered the park from the east gate and was struck with how much it reminded her of an English landscape garden, all informal, curved walkways, and things assorted at random through the grounds, as opposed to the traditional French formal garden with its symmetry and attempt to impose order upon nature. Something that was proving increasingly futile, Annabel thought. She walked the perimeter of the grounds, past statues of Chopin and Guy de Maupissant and past the bizarre follies — miniature replicas of the Great Pyramids, a Dutch Windmill, a Chinese fort. She stopped by a pond that was rimmed by a colonnade of Corinthian pillars and took a seat on one of the green benches that sat facing the water.

Annabel's concentration wandered as she watched a toddler chasing the pigeons that pecked at the floor. Her nanny — Annabel presumed she was a nanny, she didn't look anything like the girl and Annabel had noticed several very well appointed houses situated around the park, the sort of houses with live-in staff — was being given the run around by the little girl. Every time the woman called a halt to the girl's game, she would pick her up and carry her back to a bench with a pram parked next to it. She would sit the girl down, root around in the bottom of the buggy, but by the time she'd extracted the girls coat and hat she was off again, kicking at the birds and giggling furiously. Annabel couldn't help but laugh. She was so swept up in action that Annabel didn't notice the young woman bustling towards her, frantically rearranging a silk scarf that was wrapped around her neck.

'Sorry, sorry! Hi, hi, hi — did you get my email? Horrible morning. No alarm. No hot water. No nothing...' the woman paused, 'Annabel?'

Annabel looked at the woman in front of her. She carried an air of scruffiness that, given her important job, could only speak of old money. No normal person would get away with such an unkempt appearance in a professional setting. Her hair was tied up in a wild knot on top of her head, held together loosely by a motley assortment of scrunchies and hair grips. She wore a tailored double-breasted navy suit jacket, crumpled, with contrasting chino trousers, and flat pumps. She tossed the phone she was carrying inside the voluminous designer handbag that made it look like she was dragging around a builder's bucket.

'Hi,' Annabel said, snapping out of her dressing down of the woman, 'I guess you must be Chloé?'

'Yes! Yes, of course, sorry — terribly rude of me. Hello, shall we walk?'

Annabel agreed, and the two began to walk towards the north gate, past the rotunda that served as the park warden's accommodation, Chloé talking a mile a minute. Her English was good. From what Annabel knew already about her, she worked across international borders so she assumed that's where she'd picked it up. It was very heavily accented, though, and when Chloé got particularly excited, Annabel started to lose what was being said. 'So you've already spoken to Éloïse, I guess, so you know a bit about what we're up to?'

'Enlighten me — I'd love to hear it from you.'

'Sure, fine,' Chloé said, 'Well, Éloïse and her pals are concerned with the wide-angle stuff on illegal trafficking. Trying to raise public awareness, get government on board all that sort of thing. And they're also literally providing aid to the people who're caught up in the trafficking. Horrible business: stuffed into the backs of lorries, no food or water, taking halfway across the world when most of them haven't been more than ten miles from home. Especially not for days, months, years. And those sea crossings...' she paused for a moment, 'Well, we've all seen the pictures in the papers haven't we? It's disgusting. A blot on the page of humanity.' Chloé flailed her arms as she spoke, emphasising her emotions with wild waves of her hands. They were walking down a wide boulevard, towards Chloé's offices, Annabel presumed. The city was in full flow. People queued at coffee shops for their morning fix, cars and mopeds filled the streets. Yesterday's rain had vanished without a trace, leaving behind clear blue skies and a crispness in the air that felt good on Annabel's face.

'Anyway, so those guys are handling that stuff, which is where we cross over. Come on, we have to go through here. I've booked us a conference room.'

They'd arrived at Chloé's office now, a large glass-fronted building that stuck out like a sore thumb against the historical architecture that surrounded it. Annabel followed Chloé through the main lobby towards the security checkpoint. Chloé approached the desk and arranged a guest pass for Annabel, which the officious woman at the desk printed and placed inside a plastic lanyard. She leaned forward and clipped it to Annabel's jacket. Chloé cast a glance at Annabel and rolled her eyes, smiling.

They made their way through the security point, placing their bags in plastic trays on the conveyor belt and passing them through the scanner. This level of security was increasingly common in office buildings across the globe. Annabel worked freelance now, but when she had been on the payroll, she'd suffered this sort of treatment daily.

The two women assembled their items again, stuffing electrical devices back into bags, and made their way to the bank of elevators at the rear of the lobby.

'Such a stupid system,' Chloé said as she swiped her ID card over the central console, 'You have to swipe in, say what floor you want and then it directs you to a certain elevator. I guess it makes the process more efficient — the computer knows how many people it can get up and down the building in as few trips as possible — but sometimes you get stuck here waiting. Can't beat a button, if you ask me.'

They made their way up to Chloé's office in relative silence, Chloé checking her phone and occasionally talking to Annabel in a distracted way about nothing too important. Clearly she was cautious about being overheard.

Alighting on their floor, Chloé bustled through yet another open plan office to a bank of meeting rooms at the back. It was a significant improvement on the one she'd sat in back at Éloïse's office. Chloé interacted with a touchscreen set into a wall and swiped her card again. There was a satisfying clunk as the door unlocked and they made their way in. Chloé held the door open for Annabel, casting her eyes around the room as she closed it behind them. It struck Annabel as being overboard. Despite Chloé being late for their meeting, they were still early by normal standards — there were only a few people in the office. One guy sat at his desk, playing with his phone as he sipped his morning coffee. Another man at the far end of the room was kitted out in full, bright cycling lycras, helmet still on — Annabel hoped he'd be making use of the shower facilities. She'd sat next to far too many sweaty London cyclists in her time in newsrooms who'd apparently deemed it unnecessary to apply deodorant after their miles long commute.

The conference room had all the latest hi-tech equipment. Conference phones were planted in the middle of solid wood desks, a central hub sprouted with wires and cables for every possible data connection you might need to make, wide-screen monitors on the wall waited, ready to display graphs and charts and bullet-pointed presentation material wirelessly.

'So,' Annabel began again, after they'd arranged themselves in the office. Annabel's bag had stayed shut, Chloé had made pains to point out this conversation was strictly off the record.

'So,' Chloé echoed, 'So what all this boils down to is that I've read your stuff before. I saw that story about the Anaia brothers. I want to come forward. I have everything you need to blow this story up.'

'Let's not get ahead of ourselves here,' Annabel said, 'What exactly are you blowing the whistle on? Why don't you start by telling me a little about what you do here.'

'I'm involved in development schemes with academies in developing nations. I'm on... I was on... the North West Africa team, working mainly in what at one point in our country's despicable history would have been called 'French West Africa': Ivory Coast, Benin, Mali, Nigeria. I essentially oversaw the visa processes for when promising players come to France for trials. I'm sure Éloïse filled you in on all the problems that arise out of that scenario? There are, as you know, lots of well-meaning initiatives that seek to get young boys — and girls in some cases, but it's mainly boys — over from the African continent to play football in Europe. Academies over there, in Nigeria, Ivory Coast, Senegal, all seek to pick out their best talents and ship them over here under the auspices of local clubs and such, for trials at said clubs. We're tasked with checking and accrediting these organisations in Africa, to ensure that everything is above board. That no families are selling their children, that no fake agents are skimming from the top, that the kids who don't make it find their way home. You know, such is life — not everyone can play football for a living — but as much as it's our job to try to 'convert' as many trials as we can into successful players, it's also our duty to make sure that the kids who don't make it don't get dropped like a sack of flaming shit... if you'll pardon the expression. Obviously in most cases, the teams are on board with this — it's bad optics to be seen to be adding to the homeless problem on Paris' streets by tossing out less than perfect footballers into the street.'

There was a deep cynicism in everything Chloé said, a sarcasm that spoke to years of working within a human meat-grinder where young men were commodities to be exchanged over and over again until their physical prowess was spent.

'Anyway, so kids having their hopes dashed is obviously completely tragic, but at least they have a way out. They entered the country legitimately. They've got their passports, their travel documents. In most cases we also do follow up work to try to place them back at home. If not playing, then on staff. But then behind all these, behind the glossy picture, is a lot more. Some of the organisations that crop up back in Africa are less than kosher. You know how it is, when there is money there is always someone trying to make more... usually to the detriment of others. They're taking international funding to get set up, and fabricating contacts in Europe. Fake agents, fake intermediaries, fake trials. They send scouts out to the projects, to scoop up kids on false pretences, promising trials that don't exist. They go to these kids and their families, and they take their money, their life savings. They pay for flights, they get the kids into the countries legitimately, but then as soon as they're here these people — the agents, the go-betweens -- completely vanish. Poof.' Chloé flicked open a fist to emulate an explosion.

'It's basically organised crime, but they don't get picked up because now and then they'll have a hit: "Hey," they say, "It's tough becoming a footballer, they can't all make it." The difference between what they do and what we do is that we make sure the kids get back home.'

'But how is this not picked up in Europe? I'm presuming we're talking about high-ranking organisations here? How are they letting it continue?'

'Ignorance. Wilful ignorance mostly. A mix of that, and certain individuals at these organisations who receive financial incentive to sweep things under the rug. That's what I think I've found — who holds the broom.'

'Of course,' Annabel said, 'So there are people at this end falsifying records, sneaking kids in alongside the ones who really do have trials, so they can what... make some money, and have a fresh supply of labour to help maintain their homes?'

'You're not far off, yes.'

'And what exactly is it that you think you've found?'

'I noticed some... oversights, should we say?'

'What sort of oversights?' Annabel asked.

Chloé took a moment to choose her words.

'Exactly that. Oversights. Things that had been ignored. Red tape that had been cut. Certain organisations in developing nations — it's not worth mentioning them at this point — were being allowed to enter the system without passing through the appropriate checks and balances we'd put in place.'

'How would that happen?' Annabel asked the obvious question, spurring Chloé on. She already knew the answer.

'Everything we do here is signed off at board level. Which means, I suspect, that someone at board level is involving themselves. When I brought up the discrepancies, I'd found they completely shut me down. They pulled me out of work, forced me into sabbatical for a few weeks and then eventually pulled me up before the board. Judge, jury and executioner. I was reassigned, and told in no uncertain terms to drop my line of enquiry or else I'd better find alternative employment. I rocked the boat.'

'I'm guessing that you didn't stop looking?' said Annabel, smiling as she found some kinship with Chloé. Annabel's doggedness had got her into trouble with her superiors on more than one occasion.

'Correct,' Chloé said, 'I did not. I kept digging. You know what they say; follow the money? Well I did just that. Obviously there was no money changing hands over the table, so it was a case of looking at each of the board members. Most were clean as a whistle. But one — Georges Pepin — he'd been racking up a lot of air miles. Flying between Paris and Lagos, Accra, Addis Ababa... you get the idea. He'd kept his travel out of the company diary, but he'd added it to his private calendar, look...' She pulled a sheet of paper from her bag and thrust it at Annabel. On it was a series of calendar events with flight numbers. In the last six months alone, Pepin had made several trips abroad.

'I won't ask how you got access to his personal calendar,' Annabel said.

'Let's just say his assistant owed me a favour,' Chloé responded, a twinkle in her eye.

'I will just say, Chloé, it's hardly damning evidence — "Man who collaborates with football academies in Africa flies to Africa" is hardly a headline.'

'Thanks,' Chloé said, with a heavy dose of sarcasm, 'Of course I understand that, which is why I didn't stop with just his calendar. I cross-referenced his travel dates with his expense accounts. Everyone has access to them — part of one of these well-meaning transparency initiatives. You'd expect there to be a decent sized bill. If he was on official work business, he'd be meeting dignitaries, ambassadors, CEOs — there would be lunches, dinners, cars. That's not to mention private security. But there's nothing. Now, Pepin might like people to think he's a decent guy, but it's a bit of a stretch to suggest that he'd be funding his business trips out of his own pocket isn't it?' Annabel nodded in agreement. 'And, so, the logical next step must be that the money is coming from somewhere else. Ever since the 2015 scandal everyone has been on an insanely tight leash with stuff like that. We're not allowed to take anything from anyone. No chocolates, no wine, no flowers. And definitely no cash. It makes me so mad. He's so gauche with the whole thing. We all know how much it gets paid. It's a lot, but let me tell you, it isn't enough to be walking around in Brioni suits, stinking of Tom Ford aftershave, Rolex dangling from his wrist...it's such a cliche!'

Annabel jolted as Chloé slammed her hand down on the table between them.

'Context is everything, Annabel. Taken individually, the clothes, the extra cash... they don't mean a lot, but combined, they point to one thing. It goes deeper than his just turning a blind eye to a few academies. It's not just payments under the table to get around Visa issues. Those organisations have to run on a certain level of legitimacy. But I'm certain he's involved in the darker side of things as well. Éloïse would have told you, there is a criminal element. Some of the guys who show up here... well, they're terrifying, Annabel. Thugs. He's not only taking a kicker from the organisations for helping them out, but he's in league with criminal gangs, with people smugglers. These guys, they don't even pretend it's above board. They smuggle people over to Italy and then up through Europe, all the time promising bigger and better things in Rome, Berlin, Paris, but of course it never even remotely existed. I'm sure the people they bring over know it doesn't exist, but they cling onto whatever small amount of hope they have. But when they get here, they're robbed, beaten, stripped of the falsified documents their thousand dollar 'ticket' from home cost, and left cold on the streets. A few days later these gangsters come back, offer them a warm bed, a hot meal, and then that's it. Job done. A new slave to do their bidding. One who's too terrified to speak out, who can't got to the cops for fear of deportation... slavery didn't die, Annabel, they just re-badged it. It is a tragedy of epic proportion and everyone is ignoring it. No more.'

'Okay, okay,' Annabel cut Chloé off before she got more carried away, 'But you know as well as I do that for anything to happen we're going to need proof. Information that can corroborate your claims. People are going to want more than just some hearsay about a guy wearing too nice a suit.'

'Ah, but I do have it... at least, I know where to start looking,' Chloé said, conspiratorially, 'I have his assistant onside, like I told you — we broke into his em--'

'Chloé, I need to say this. What you're doing is very illegal. This could end with you not just losing your job, but facing prosecution.'

'People are being torn from their homes, shoved onto inflatable dinghies to cross oceans, left to fend for themselves on foreign streets, all because some guy wants a kickback to pay for his new pool. It's unacceptable. And it won't stop unless people know about it. I have had enough. It's time to speak out. Like Manning, like Snowden, like Assan—'

Chloé's voice was raised, and Annabel was beginning to wish they'd kept their conversation outside. She looked through the glass through to the open plan office and noticed several heads cocked towards them, furtive glances keeping check on them. 'Georges' assistant assures me he's seen emails that support everything. This all started as a bit of lunchtime gossip, but when Robert did a bit of digging, he came up with gold. Almost literally. A paper trail that proves Georges is taking gifts from the African academies.' Chloé cast a furtive glance through the window back into the office before digging her hand into her inside pocket. 'Here,' she said, and placed a thumb drive on the table, 'I've not had a chance to look at this yet, but it's all on there, everything.'

Annabel weighed up her options. It didn't take long. She wasn't committing to anything by taking a look at the files. She had been in the game long enough to know how to protect her sources. If nothing came from the data, so be it, she would thank Chloé and move on. If there was something there, though, some suggestion not just of Georges Pepin's penchant for a backhander, but his active involvement with criminal gangs gave the story a bit more spice.

'There's one more thing,' Chloé said, sensing the end of the meeting, 'Something Robert said to me when I asked him to print out Georges' calendar. He said that he'd been taking a lot of calls from someone inside the Sports Minister's office, and that every time he put a call through, Georges closed his door and made Robert leave. I think there might be someone in government who Georges is close to who is allowing these people to slip through the immigration net — the kids from the academies and the ones who are smuggled here.'

'But to what end?'

'Money, Annabel. It's always about money. Either that, or the gangs hold something over someone. People in the public eye have a lot to lose. Their career, their family, their power... it's easy to manipulate that.'

Even if there was half a truth in what Chloé said about Georges being in league with a government official, she knew she would get green-lit to run the story. As long as the evidence was there and it was irrefutable. The game was afoot.

7

Afam hadn't got more than a few hours' sleep that night. The cold water he splashed on his face the next morning did little to blow away the tiredness he felt. It ached in his bones. It had been very late by the time he had got home and he had ended up arguing with his mother.

'You are the man of the house, Afam. You need to take some responsibility. You can't just be gallivanting with your friends all night,' his mother had said. He couldn't bring himself to tell her the real reason he had been late. For one thing, he wasn't sure how she would react, but also he felt ashamed. He had let Sam trick him. Had let Sam touch him. Afam didn't feel like the man of the house, he felt like a little boy. A foolish little boy.

A gentle knocking on the glass of his window stopped him spiralling too deeply into the memory. He moved across his small room in a few steps and looked through the windowpane, narrowing his eyes to focus on the dark outside. The sun had yet to properly rise but he could make out Leye's face. Afam couldn't hide his confusion. He held up two fingers, two minutes, and hurriedly threw on his clothes before moving outside.

'Leye, what are you doing here this early? Did your house burn down?' Afam joked through the darkness.

'I need to talk to you,' Leye didn't return the good humour.

'Not you as well?' Afam said.

'What do you mean?'

'Nothing... just my mom gave me a thick ear last night for coming home late. Hold on, let me grab my things and you can walk me to work. Are you going to school? They won't understand what's happening if you turn up on time.' Afam returned to his room and picked up his bag. He could feel the weight of the football boots from Sam as he slung the pack over his shoulder. As he turned to leave, Iman was making her way out of her room towards the kitchen.

'Morning, brother,' she smiled at him through half-closed eyes as she poured a glass of water from a five-gallon jug.

'Morning, sis. I'm going to work. Be good, I'll see you later.' He planted a kiss on her forehead and she swatted at him.

'I'm always good. It's what I do. One of us has to,' she called out after him as he went out through the front door.

* * *

'So, what's so important that you dragged your carcass out of bed this early? Your house is still standing, you didn't wet the bed... so what?' Afam was putting on a brave face. He desperately wanted to tell Leye about what had happened the night before but he couldn't quite bring himself to do it yet.

Leye stayed quiet, letting his friend's jibes roll over him. Afam could almost see the cogs whirring as Leye chewed over what he was trying to say. Leye took a deep breath, exhaled.

'I don't think we should see Sam any more. He is not a good man.' Finally Leye spoke, his words puncturing the tension between the two boys. Afam felt his heartbeat increase. His palms felt cold, clammy.

'What do you mean?' he laughed, pretending to pass it off though inside his head screamed, desperate to reveal what had happened the night before.

'He is not the good Christian he claims to be,' Leye seemed in physical pain as he pushed the words out. He paused, weighing up his next words, 'The other night, after he'd dropped you and Iman off, he drove me home afterwards...'

Afam couldn't speak. He knew what Leye was about to say. How could he not? He wanted to tell him to stop, that he didn't need to carry on, that he understood. But he felt paralysed.

'But we didn't go straight there. He started talking to me about a foundation that he ran through the church that gave grants to young people who want to get into business. We carried on driving, I was telling him all about my ideas and he was being really positive about everything. We got all the way out to near the prison in Kirikiri before I realised we were a long way from home. I could see the blue roofs. He pulled the car over in some back street and let me keep talking. He just stared at me while I spoke, but his face had changed. I can't tell you how. He was like an animal. He--'

Afam had stopped walking. He stood in the middle of the road staring off into the middle distance.

'What's wrong?' Leye noticed the solitary tear on Afam's cheek. He didn't need to ask. The anger that had risen in his voice as he spoke about the evening with Sam instantly abated as he sensed the pain in his friend. 'No?' Afam's nod was almost imperceptible.

'That fucking bastard!' Leye shouted, his whole body tensing as he hurled a flurry of curses into the dawn sky.

'Leye, calm down,' Afam placed a hand on his friend's back but Leye threw it off, spinning round at him.

'You tell me to calm down? When this animal roams our streets? Did he hurt you?' Afam shook his head.

'But how long until he does? How long until it's a younger kid? Someone who can't fight back?' Leye was clenching his fists. He turned and walked off at pace in the opposite direction to which they'd came.

'Leye? Leye, where are you going?' Afam called out after him.

'Come on,' said Leye, without looking back once.

* * *

'Leye, what are you doing? Someone's going to see us,' Afam said. He was leaning on a gatepost, trying to look casual as he kept watch both ways down the street.

'Just a minute longer,' Leye said, his voice muffled. All Afam could see of him were his bright blue sandals, his feet poking out from underneath Sam's minibus. Afam could hear him scratching around in the dirt, the occasional snip of wire cutters. A light yellow-brown substance was pooling on the floor from beneath the car.

Afam watched as more of Leye emerged until he was clear of the underside of the car and standing in front of Afam, his school polo shirt covered in dust and debris and grease.

'What were you doing, anyway?'

'Oh, nothing,' Leye's smile was full of malice, 'Just giving our friend a scare. Hopefully he'll get the message.'

'I don't know, this seems like a terrible idea.' Afam was confused, he hadn't seen this side of his friend before. 'He didn't hurt anyone, did he?'

'Not yet,' Leye said, the force with which he said it ending that line of conversation.

Before Afam had a chance to ask any more questions, a porch light flicked on and the two boys darted out of the driveway.

Afam peeked his head around the corner and saw Sam through the screen door, standing in his underpants and a stained white t-shirt. He walked out onto the stoop and looked out onto the street, straining his neck this way and that, searching for the source of the noise he had heard.

Afam felt Leye tugging on his sleeve, but he stayed glued to the corner, watching whilst Sam gave up his search and turned to go inside. When Sam was back inside, Afam turned to Leye.

'Not a word,' Leye said, holding his finger to his lips.

'Come on,' Afam said, 'I'm going to be late for work, and you don't want to miss the once-in-a-lifetime chance to be the first one at school in the morning, do you?'

* * *

Afam had walked home alone. After the morning with Leye, he wanted some time to himself to try to clear his head. He was kicking a can down the road, his eyes focused on the middle distance as he tried to feel the can with his feet, trying to build his sense of where the ball might be without looking. As he approached home he heard a growing murmur. He looked up and saw a crowd assembled in front of him. It looked like an electricity pylon had fallen into the road but he couldn't see through the throng. He kicked the can to the side of the road and picked up the pace, heading towards the pack.

'Hello, Afam — no football for you today?'

'Hi Mrs. Adenle,' Afam greeted his neighbour, who stood at the edge of the crowd that was pushing up against a police cordon, 'What's happening?'

'Some van has come off the road,' said the woman. She wasn't looking at Afam as she spoke, instead she was craning her neck up high trying to see over the heads of the gathered crowd. 'Dead driver, white man from the church, so everyone has gone crazy. It's like Lasgidi Cops. You'd never know there was a boy in there who'd survived...'

Afam pushed his way through the crowd. At the front, holding people back, were six men in the drab green uniforms of the Nigerian Police Force. They wore black Kevlar vests with 'POLICE' emblazoned on the front. Kalashnikov assault rifles hung idly at their sides.

Thick tyre marks were etched across the road, tracing a deadly route to the rear of the van. The front of the minibus was wrapped around an electricity pole that had snapped just above where the van had impacted and was folded down on top of the car. A web of power cables splayed out, deadly, like the tentacles of a Man o' War. The windscreen had shattered, a white sheet draped over the drivers' side, obscuring the view. A crew of firefighters stood at the side of the vehicle, deliberating how best to extricate the body from the wreck. Afam could make out the markings on the side of the van: 'Preach the Word'.

An ambulance was pulled up alongside the crashed car, and a young boy sat by the back door. Afam recognised him from Iman's class. The boy was covered in a foil blanket, sipping from a bottle of water whilst a team of paramedics attended him. He let them prod and poke him, looking for dilation in his pupils, signs of head trauma. Afam hoped that they didn't have to dig out any other sort of trauma, either.

People jostled Afam from either side, phones held aloft, desperate to get the exclusive angle that might get them onto the evening news. Voices clamoured, shouting into the receivers so loudly that might not have even bothered using the phone at all. But Afam could barely hear a word being said. The voices smashed into one another in his head creating such a din that it felt strangely silent. He could hear the deep echo in his chest as he drew breath in. Out. Maintained a steady rhythm as he stared at the scene before him, keeping his heart beat under control. He felt cold despite the warmth of the afternoon. Leye. He needed to get to Leye.

He felt a hand grip his arm.

'Take it easy, Afam,' Leye's voice cut through the tumult of the crowd, 'Let's get out of here.'

Afam allowed Leye to lead him away from the cordon. The two boys weaved through the crowd, which parted and reconvened around them, flowing like water to fill the space they left in their wake.

'Tell me that wasn't Sam--'

'Shh, not here,' Leye cut Afam off, not turning around to speak to him, keeping his gaze fixed ahead as he ducked through the throng.

As they broke through the back of the crowd, Leye led Afam round the back of a row of houses. He finally turned to Afam, eyes wide. He was trying to look calm, but Afam saw fear in his friend's eyes.

'What are we going to do?' Afam asked.

'What are we going to do?' Leye responded, his brow furrowing, 'We're not going to do anything.'

'But... Sam, he's dead... we--'

'We didn't do anything,' Leye cut him off, staring hard into Afam's eyes. 'This has nothing to do with us. You should be talking about what he did,' Leye nodded his head back towards the accident, 'You think it was just you? Just me? Just that kid back there? If this was anything to do with us, which it isn't,' Leye held onto the lie for dear life, 'Then we did the world a favour.'

Afam was seeing a new side to Leye — something cold, violent, inhumane. Afam was racked with guilt, he couldn't get the image of Sam's lifeless body out of his head. The shell-shocked boy staring out into space as he was prodded and poked. The memory of the previous night by the water crept into his thoughts. He had escaped relatively unscathed, but the change he had seen in Sam in that moment had changed Afam fundamentally. He had liked Sam, had trusted him. But Sam had destroyed all of that. And now he lay dead, tossed through the windshield of his car, all because Afam went along with Leye's stupid plan. He could have tried harder to convince him not to do it. Could have pretended someone was coming to force Leye to stop what he had done. Did that make him a murderer? He hadn't pulled the trigger, but he hadn't done enough, hadn't done anything, to stop Leye pulling it.

'Afam,' Leye broke Afam free from his thought spiral, 'We are going to need to get out of town for a while. Just until this all disappears.'

'What are you talking about? I can't leave!' Afam couldn't believe what Leye was suggesting. His family relied on his income — his mom wouldn't survive on her own. Iman would have to drop out of school. Would have to start working to put food on the table to keep herself and the babies, Azi and Ade, fed. As the second eldest, she'd have to pick up whatever Afam left behind. He couldn't let that happen. He couldn't betray her.

'We just need to stay out of the way for a bit. You know what it's like here. School was already suspicious of me when I turned up early. Who knows who else saw us? You know what this place is like!' Leye threw his hands out, indicating the world around them. 'What's worse — disappearing for a few weeks, or ending up in prison for the rest of your life? Where would your family be then?'

'This is crazy!' Neither option felt like a choice to Afam. If he ran away, it would leave his family in a very precarious position, if he stayed, and he and Leye were found out, then he would spend the rest of his life in jail. 'Where the hell would we go?'

'We aren't going anywhere...' Afam frowned at Leye's response, 'I can go and stay with my cousin. Maybe you should talk to Moses?'

'Are you kidding me? Last week you're telling me 'Oh, this guy's a crook Afam, don't trust him...' and now you're telling me to put my life in his hands? You've lost your mind!'

'Fine, stay then. But I'm gone.' Leye turned and walked away from Afam, back out of the alley, and disappeared into the sea of people still milling around the crash site. Afam went to call him back, but thought better of drawing further attention to himself. He sat on an upturned bottle crate and stared into the dusty ground in front of him, turning over his choices in his head. After a while he got up, slung his bag over his shoulder and trudged through to the street.

The crowd had more or less dispersed by now, a few latecomers still hung around, catching up on the gossip, providing their own angles to rumours about the American missionary who only ever had boys in his car. Afam was deaf to the whispers as he made his way home. It felt like he was having to drag himself every step of the way. He didn't know how he could look his mother in the eye, his brothers. Iman.

As Afam rounded the corner to his street, their house came into view and he could see Iman through the window. She was holding her baby brother in her arms and dancing around, holding onto the hand of the other twin as they sang and played drums on any surface they could find. His heart ached to be able to walk through the door, to be greeted by the smiles of his family, to add his voice to the chorus. But he couldn't. He was marked. Tainted. He couldn't bring what was following him home to them.

He tightened the straps of his rucksack and kept on walking.

* * *

Afam waited until long after dark before he turned back home. The street was still, the night air carried the sounds of the city. The traffic noise was a gentle, distant scratching, blasts of car horns and engines revving punctured the nocturnal hum.

The window shutters had been pulled shut, the garden furniture stacked away under the porch. Afam trod lightly as he approached the front door, lifted the latch with as much delicacy as he could muster, winced at the squeal of the rusty hinges.

The house was dark inside and Afam did his best not to make any noise as he made his way through the kitchen towards his room. He dug out his kit bag and started stuffing clothes in, not stopping to think about what he might need. He had no passport to pack. With clothes bulging out of his bag, he went to the bathroom and picked up his toothbrush and comb, stuffing them inside the pack. One of his brothers called out in his sleep and Afam's ears pricked to the noise, hoping the cry wouldn't wake his mother. After a minute, stood stock still in the hallway that connected all the rooms in the house, he let out a breath he didn't realise he had been holding and walked through to the kitchen and poured himself a cup of water from the bottle on the side.

'Going somewhere, brother?'

Iman.

Afam turned sharply, spilling water down his front as he faced his sister. He looked at his bag, looked back to her. Tried to read her questioning gaze.

'I...I..' She held her palm up to him as he tried to bumble through a lie.

'Don't even bother — you're such a terrible liar, Afam,' Iman rolled her eyes, her head shook slightly.

'I just need to go away for a few days. It won't be long and then I'll be back. Please don't ask questions. I just need you to trust me, okay?'

Iman sensed the sadness in her brother and adopted a less teasing position.

'Are you okay? Is it Leye? What's he done now? You're not in trouble with those stupid boys at the pitches are you?'

'Please, Iman, don't. I'm fine, totally fine. Everything will be okay, I promise.'

Iman considered her brother. It was clear she wasn't going to get a straight answer out of him, and any more conversation out here in the main house risked waking her brothers.

'Fine. But just promise me you'll be safe...' she conceded, '... and that you'll come back?'

'I promise. Please, I need to go. Look after mom?' Afam grabbed his sister in a clumsy embrace. Planted a kiss on her cheek.

Iman pushed him back. 'Wait here, just a second...' She turned and went to her room. Afam heard her scrabbling around through the set of drawers next to her bed. Iman reemerged a few seconds later with a gold chain dangling from her fist.

'Take this,' she passed him the chain and Afam took it in his hand. In the dark of the kitchen he could just make out the pendant.

'It's St Jude. I found it at the market. Patron Saint of lost souls, brother. Keep it close.'

Afam wrapped his fist around the jewellery and exhaled deeply, his eyes closed. He stepped forward again and wrapped Iman in a bear hug.

A cough from their brother's room broke the moment and Iman pushed her brother away, moving back down the hall towards her room, leaving Afam standing alone in the main doorway.

'Go, Afam. Stay safe. Come home soon.'

8

Afam clutched the sheaf of documents that Moses had given him to his chest as he stood by the payphone. The wind blew sand all around him and he pulled his jacket tight against it. Even though the sun was bright in the sky, the sea breeze carried a slight chill. He pulled out the contents of the envelope. A passport, his first, and various other bureaucratic necessities that would allow him to work in France, 'If the trial goes well,' Moses had said. It felt crazy that a small bundle of papers could have cost so much money. He tried not to think about how he would begin to pay it back. He had paid a small deposit, his entire savings. It was nowhere near enough, but Moses' guy had said they could work out a payment plan for the rest. Of course, Afam didn't hold out much hope that there was a trial. Hopefully with the falsified documents, he could find a bit of work in Paris and make enough to pay Moses back and then get himself back home. He had hated lying to Iman. He knew that as soon as he spoke to Moses, he would be away for a lot longer than a few weeks, but it had seemed like his only option. Certainly it seemed the safest option.

He had left Lagos in the early morning, the sun's rays barely cresting the horizon. They had bundled him into the back of a truck and had found a place to sit amongst the various stacks of boxes filled with all manner of products. He found himself sat amongst a dozen or so others, and wondered how long they had been travelling already. Wondered what they were running from. Now and then, on the highways, the truck would pull over and the roll cage at the back would open. Afam and the others in the back would get out of the trailer and stretch their legs, gulp down water from the bottles that were handed to them, and make toilet in the most secluded place they could find. But then they were forced back inside, boxed up, hidden, out of sight as they crossed border after border. Whenever they were approaching a checkpoint, the driver would deliver sharp knocks that reverberated through the trailer and the passengers would squeeze themselves behind a false wall in the trailer. Afam closed his eyes during these moments, not wanting to catch the gaze of anyone, not wanting to see their pain, not wanting to think of the reasons they were making this journey too. Were there others here who were murderers? Criminals on the run? Or was he the rotten egg, everyone else just looking for escape, the smallest glimmer of hope for a different life. Did they all know how futile their journeys would prove?

They left the green of West Africa and made their way north, through the stark desert plains. Afam had never seen anything like it. It was so remote. He was from the city, where you couldn't look in any direction without seeing layer upon layer of people, buildings, vehicles. Where sounds and smells came at you from all directions. But out there in the desert there had been nothing. They had passed through towns and cities where people had made a life in the most inhospitable of places, but between these oases there was nothing but sand as far as the eye could see, no sound except the chug of the diesel engine that ferried them towards the port where they would take their chance on the Mediterranean.

The port town was the first time in days Afam had stepped out of the vehicle that had brought him all this way. Parked up in a back street by the water, the roll cage at the back of the truck had been raised and men, women and children unfolded from crevasses throughout the van's rear, blinking in the harsh daylight, inching out of their cocoon. Men waited, stood around the courtyard.

'The boat leaves tonight. Keep out of the way until then.' Afam hadn't seen this man before, but didn't think twice about following his orders. At least six feet tall, his head shaved razor-close, his face carried a series of pock-marks and scars that spoke less to childhood acne and more to battle scars. Part of his ear was missing, a thick keloid scar tracing the outline of teeth marks. I'd hate to see the state of the loser, thought Afam.

Afam had done as he was told, though had made good use of the anonymity a busy city provides. Around AJ City he found it hard to hide, it was a close knit community, but he only had to go a few miles in either direction and he blended into the crowd like any other kid. It was nice, sometimes, to be somewhere that nobody knew you, that nobody expected anything from you. Afam made his way out onto the streets, where he used some American dollars to buy some food from a street vendor. He had got the money from an uncle who had been to New York on business once and it had stayed under his mattress since then. The man looked at him warily as he prepared the food, stuffing shredded chicken into a flatbread with chopped salad and vegetables.

Afam hadn't eaten properly for days, and marvelled as the earthy taste of charcoal grilled chicken and spices muddled with the sweetness of pomegranate molasses. He wiped his mouth with the back of his hand and cracked open the can of soda he'd bought. As he drank, he felt the ice cold liquid revive him. It was as though he could feel the cold and the sugar working its way into his veins, sharpening him to the world around.

Afam checked his watch. It wasn't long before they would have to be on the boat. He wondered how long the crossing would be. Despite having grown up near the coast, he had never gotten used to the sea. He and his friends would often make their way to the beach at weekends outside of summer. By then, the tourists had gone home, and the hotels cared less about the locals invading their private stretch of sand. They played football, cooked on open fires and sank bottles of Hero and they would be in and out of the water. But as soon as it got above Afam's waist he would head back in. He had hated the feeling of weightlessness, though being spurred on by his friends, had continued to swim out from the shore. The further he went, the more he lost sight of the seabed. Inside he had been panicking, he hated not knowing what was around him, next to him. Beneath. As the others had continued playing he had made his excuses and doggy-paddled back to shore, shaking himself off as his feet touched dry land. He towelled off and crashed down into the sand, turning to see Leye and the rest of their friends horsing around, dunking one another beneath the waves. It didn't look so far out from there, he had felt embarrassed at how scared he had been, but still he had been happy to be lying back on the sand.

Afam crushed the now empty can in his hand and perched the litter on a teetering pile that spilled from a trashcan. He nodded thanks to the stall owner, who glared at him, unblinking. Taking his cue to move on, Afam headed back towards the truck he had called home this past few days. The driving had been non-stop. Instead of making stop-overs where the driver would catch up on sleep, they had teams of two drivers who swapped whenever they had to refuel, then drove for hours straight. As they crossed border checkpoints, the teams would switch out — the people who had started Afam on his journey were not the ones completing it. A few of his cabin mates milled around the perimeter of their hiding place. There was a mother with her two young children, one swaddled against her chest, the other, a girl, climbing on broken packing boxes, peeking around corners and through the broken panes of glass in the sides of the buildings that surrounded them.

Afam laughed as she repeatedly tried and failed to catch a pigeon that kept returning to peck at the surrounding floor.

The girl bent low, arms outstretched, creeping up behind the bird as it pecked dumbly at the floor. Each time she got within a few feet her eyes would go wide, her excitement barely contained. Afam watched as she crouched as low as she could then pounced forward like a wildcat, flinging her arms through the air towards her prey. The bird was always one step ahead of her and would leap up in a flurry of noise, dust and feathers to take refuge on an overhanging electrical wire, its vacant stare darting around to assess whether the danger had passed.

On this attempt, the girl had landed hard and scraped her knee. She let out a small mewl, but her mother swooped over and quelled any histrionics before they'd started — the small family had become all too practised in keeping quiet, not alerting anyone to their presence. Afam wondered what their story was, where they had come from. What they had left behind that meant crossing the open sea in a dinghy was the better option.

As the commotion died down, the men returned. One man looked at the assembled refugees, drew hard on his cigarette, exhaled with purpose.

'We go now,' he said, 'This way. Follow.'

Afam approached the girl's mother as she struggled with the meagre belongings that accompanied them. Things for the baby, mainly, and a few clothes.

'Here,' he said, and reached out for the rucksack. The woman snatched it back and Afam let go in shock. He held out his hand in a placating gesture. 'Please. I can help.'

She looked at him, deep into him, and considered for a moment. A small smile cracked, and she handed the bag over to Afam.

'Afam,' he said, tapping his chest open-palmed.

'Awusi,' the woman replied, mimicking the gesture.

Afam pointed to the girl, who was now holding her mother's hand.

'Effia,' Awusi said, smiling, and then patted the head of the baby strapped to her chest, 'Kojo.' Kojo squirmed against his mother but his eyes stayed firmly shut.

'Let's go,' came a voice from across the yard and Afam slung the backpack over his shoulder, taking Effia's other hand in his and walking the family towards the bay.

***

Afam and the others sat beneath a jetty on the beach as night fell. The longer they lingered, the more Afam had been lulled by the sound of the sea lapping at the sand, the soft rolling thunder that announced the coming of a new wave. Afam and Effia had passed the time by concocting an elaborate game using various pieces of flotsam and wrack that they found in the sand. Afam could never seem to learn the rules to the game, which seemed to be in constant flux, with Effia more often than not declaring herself the winner. Awusi and Kojo rested nearby, the mother grabbing sleep whilst the baby did.

The days were longer than at home, and it felt as though they had waited ages for the sun to set, longer still for the noise of life to die down as the city gradually went to sleep. When he finally saw the dinghy being dragged ashore, Afam checked his watch. 2:30 AM. Afam knew nothing about seafaring, but he had enough common sense to be scared by what he saw. A twenty-foot inflatable raft with an outboard motor strapped to the back. It didn't seem big enough to fit ten people in. There were fifty of them waiting under the jetty. The men who had guarded them by the van approached then, waving their AK47 rifles around, their voices hushed but forceful.

'Come. Quickly. Take this.' Someone handed Afam a jerry can, the diesel smell wafting into his nose at the liquid sloshed around inside. 'Don't drop it!' The man who had handed it to him laughed and passed another canister to one of the men behind. Afam quickly took off his belt and tied one end to the handle of the canister, the other he tied around his wrist. The hard edge of the cheap leather cut into his wrist.

He felt a hand in his and looked to see Effia standing beside him, eyes wide at the man brandishing the gun.

'Come on,' he said, 'You can sit next to me.' The two walked over to the dinghy and Afam lifted the girl up into the middle of the vessel. He placed the jerry can of diesel inside the boat and turned back to the beach and Effia squealed.

'Relax, I'm going to get your mom,' Afam said, and carried on up the beach to where Awusi had just finished changing Kojo. She was struggling with him as she swaddled him inside the Kanga she had wrapped around her. The baby wriggled and bucked, enjoying the game. He was the only one who laughed, though. Without saying anything, Afam bent and took the bag from the sand beside Awusi, and offered his other hand to her. She took Afam's hand and hoisted herself up. They operated like a small family unit, as though they had practised this routine a thousand times before.

Effia's worry turned to a smile as she saw her mother and brother being escorted by Afam back across to her. The three travellers took their position on the craft, Awusi sitting in front of her daughter, infant son wrapped tight against her chest again, suckling for comfort, his eyes closed, face a picture of serenity that belied the situation. Afam picked up the jerry can and re-tied it to his arm and took up position behind Effia. Everyone shifted and leaned against one another, some lying on the floor like sardines, others sitting with their legs dangling over the sides, holding onto ropes that traced the gunwale.

'Do we have life jackets?' Afam asked to the nearest smuggler in English.

'Yes, yes. You will get one. Don't worry, my friend,' said the man, flashing a gold-toothed grin, 'The driver has a satellite phone as well.'

'How long does it take?'

'A few hours. You will be safe on dry land very soon. In Italy, a very beautiful country.'

'Do we hav—'

'No more questions. Time to go.' The man cut him off, throwing several more cans of fuel into the hull of the boat. 'Hold on tight!'

As he spoke, several of the smugglers heaved the boat back into the water. The pilot ripped the starter cord of the outboard motor and the two-stroke engine roared to life. The boat lurched as the engine throttled forward and the driver piloted them in a tight circle, pointing the nose out to sea. It was the first time Afam had noticed the great wide expanse, he had been too busy worrying about home, ensuring Awusi and her children were okay. In the dead of night, it was hard to make out the line where the sky met the sea. It seemed like endless black, the light of the moon and pinpricks of starlight no match for the endless stretch of the Mediterranean. They headed into the abyss, the engine struggling against the load. There was no turning back now.

9

At first there had been a sense of relief amongst the travellers as they realised they were on the last leg of their ordeal. Admittedly, it was the most dangerous part, but it signalled the end — an end to cramped spaces, to strangers with guns. It was the only thing that stood between them and a better life except immigration authorities.

As the sun rose, the glass-still water — perfect for tourists on beaches or people sailing their sloops out on day trips — shimmered in the early morning light. After half a day cutting through the open waters, it became clear to all on board that the 'few hours' they had promised them had been wildly inaccurate. The smuggler had not lied to Afam. The journey across the Mediterranean had taken them hours, but anything takes hours depending on how you present it. They had sailed in and out of days. The longer the journey wore on, the more cramped the boat had felt.

At first, as they came round to the fact that they would not be going anywhere fast, the people came together, pooling the meagre resources they had brought: bottles of water, candy bars, a few bits of fruit. But still anticipating only a few more hours of travel, the provisions were soon gone and the sense of relief had given way to other things. Fear, claustrophobia, hunger, thirst.

With nothing to give shade, the sun beat down on them all and some of the stronger travellers took off their shirts and constructed a makeshift canopy. The smell of fifty or so people huddled under the sunshade mingled with the hot rubber of the dinghy and the stink of the diesel fumes and the combination of thick atmosphere and scorching Mediterranean heat caused some people to fall unconscious. The people around them didn't bother trying to wake them. One less mouth to feed until they reached dry land.

Afam felt terrible for having kept the water that Awusi had brought aboard hidden from the others. But she had two mouths to feed. It was a perfectly reasonable thing to have done. When he thought no one was looking, he would smuggle her sips, and to the children, Effia and Kojo.

Now they were out at sea, Afam felt freer to talk aloud. There was very little else to do. He and Awusi found a common tongue in English, though Afam's was better than hers.

'So, it's just you and the two kids? Is there someone waiting for you on the other side?' he asked, not realising how leading his question sounded to Awusi's ears.

'Their father went away for work,' she explained, 'But I haven't heard from him in months. He doesn't send money home for us. I don't know whether he's dead or living. There was nothing there for us. I used what savings we had to pay for this, begged help from the people in my village. These men, they tell me there is work on the other side. I will send money back home to pay everyone back. Hopefully we'll get to go home, eventually.'

'Same here,' Afam lied, 'I've got a trial at a top football team in Paris.'

Awusi raised both eyebrows, 'Hey, big man! Don't forget us when you're famous, eh? Tell me, do most footballers get to the top riding banana boats across dangerous seas?'

Afam laughed at Awusi's obvious sarcasm. She reminded him a little of Iman.

'I suppose they don't, no. But I have to take every chance I get. And anyway, I had to get away from Lagos for a while.'

When she pressed him on the reasons why, Afam made poor excuses he was sure Awusi didn't believe and after a while she dropped the subject and the two settled into companionable chit-chat about their lives, eventually falling into comfortable silence. It wasn't too long before Effia broke it.

'Play a game with me, Afam?' she said.

'You and your games — why do I always lose?'

'How do I know? You need to practice more.'

Afam smiled and left Awusi snoozing, sat up against the side of the dinghy, and shuffled over to Effia who had constructed an elaborate game using debris that she'd found on the boat floor.

'Okay, so how do I win?' he asked the girl, who beamed as she began to explain the rules.

* * *

Afam woke to the sound of yelling. He rubbed at his eyes, shielded them with his hand before opening them a crack, letting his pupils get used to the blazing sun. He blinked, forcing his eyelids open fully to see the source of the commotion. Two people were yelling back towards the driver, who shook his head, not paying any attention to the pleas coming from both men. Afam didn't recognise them from before — they must have joined the group at the docks before they'd left.

One man was gesturing out to the open water and Afam craned his neck to see what he was pointing at. A few hundred metres off of the back of the boat he could see movement in the water, a dark shape bobbing on the surface, hands waving desperately before switching to a frantic doggy paddle in pursuit of the vessel. Afam's eyes widened with horror.

'Hey!' he said to the driver, 'There's someone in the water. We have to go back.'

'You're welcome to go in after him,' came the reply, 'I have a schedule to keep. Besides, relax: one less mouth to feed, one less person to drag across this...' The driver gestured to the endless blue around them.

Afam couldn't believe what he was hearing, campaigned again for the driver to turn around, but the boat chugged resolutely forward.

'What happened?' Afam turned to the two men next to him.

'He fell asleep,' said one, 'Passed out and slipped off the side of the boat.' He pointed an accusing finger in the direction of the driver, 'And he won't stop the boat to get him.'

'Please,' Afam tried with the driver again, 'At least let us go in and get him back.'

The driver thought for a moment.

'Fine,' he said, 'He can go in after him.' He pointed at the man who'd spoken to Afam.

Without hesitation, the man dived off the side of the boat and swam towards his friend. He wrapped one arm around him and the two began paddling back to the boat. But as they approached, the driver accelerated, increasing the distance between the men in the water and the boat.

'What are you doing? They'll both drown,' came the voice of the second man.

'Hey, I said he could go in after him, I didn't say I'd wait.' A malicious smile crept across the driver's face as he stared directly into the man's eyes.

The other man moved towards the back of the boat and grabbed at the tiller and the boat jerked sideways as he pulled the thing hard to starboard, throwing the occupants into the side of the hull. The others who had been dozing were fully awake now, trying to make sense of the scene before them.

The driver pushed the man off and he stumbled back, tripping over some of the other passengers who were lying on the floor of the boat and falling hard on his back. The driver steadied their course and checked his bearings on a compass strapped to his wrist, as they ploughed on through the water to their final destination.

The man on the floor dragged himself back up and threw himself towards the back of the boat, enraged at the fact his friends were being left behind to drown and no doubt embarrassed by how easily his initial attempt to take control had been thrown off. This time, though, he didn't go for the tiller but directly for the driver. Sensing what was happening, the driver reached under his seat and drew a handgun. Two shots rang out, the reports echoing out into the wide open space around them. The man stopped dead in his tracks and clutched his chest, falling heavily onto his side. With great effort, he rolled onto his back and stared up into the sky, every breath bringing with it a hissing noise as blood bubbled from a wound in his chest.

The driver placed the gun in his waistband and got up from his seat at the back of the boat. He approached the man and rifled through his pockets, pocketing the few folded notes that he found. He placed two hands under the man's torso and with great effort hurled him over the side of the boat, the splash of the body entering the water masked by the screams from those on board.

'One more for the sharks,' the driver said as he wiped his bloody hands on his trousers before turning to the group of people who were now clamouring away from him, trying to gain as much distance as they could in the tiny space, 'Now, anyone else?'

The boat watched in complete silence as the man returned to his seat, checked his compass and yanked at the starter cord bringing the engine roaring back to life.

* * *

It was close to two full days before they reached the shore, Afam had kept track on his watch. After the blistering sun had begun to fall in the sky, they had removed the makeshift sunshade, putting their clothes back on to brace against the oncoming chill of the night. Afam's shirt was damp from the sea spray and he shivered as he pulled the cold, wet fabric over his back.

The crystal clear sky turned to night, the warmth of the day evaporating up into the atmosphere. Awusi and the children had huddled against one and he had wrapped himself around them all, sharing their warmth. That first night he hadn't been able to get much sleep, and had lay back staring at the night sky. He had always marvelled at old stories of sailors navigating by the stars — with so few, like there were in Lagos, how could they tell where they were going at all? But out here it became crystal clear. He had never seen such a sight. The sky resembled a backlit canopy with holes punched in it.

As dawn broke, he felt a tug at his arm and woke with a start. The smuggler, the man piloting the boat, was pulling at the jerry can that was still attached to Afam's arm. The man was caked in the same sweat and grime as those he was smuggling. He took off his sunglasses, squinting against the sun and dabbed at the sweat on his forehead with a rag that he had pulled out of his back pocket. It did little but smear the grime to new areas of his face.

'Last one,' Afam said as he undid the belt around his wrist and handed it over. Across the water Afam could make out a coastline. Hope rose in his chest.

'How long?' he asked.

'Not here,' the man pointed across to the shore, shook his head. 'Few more hours, still.'

Afam's heart sank. He watched as the man moved towards the back of the boat and began filling the motor with the fuel. Afam cast his gaze out again, feeling safer having seen dry land again.

Soon they would be safe. Effia stirred next to him and Afam lay a hand on her back, coaxing her back into sleep. He felt her breath settle again and lay back against the hull of the boat and closed his eyes. All he could do was wait.

* * *

Somehow they had managed to avoid being picked up and landed on a deserted area of the beach. The people in the boat piled out of it as soon as they reached a point in the surf where the water was waist height. Collectively, they ran for the shore and Afam watched as some of them fell down to their knees, planting kisses on the sand and praying utterances to whoever was listening.

'Stay here,' Afam said to Awusi as the motor of the boat cut out. She held the children tight, her face a mixture of relief at reaching dry land and fear at what lay ahead. Effia was peeking her head over the gunwale, excited by the commotion. Kojo slept. Afam launched himself over the side and helped tug the boat through the surf until he felt the seabed bite the bottom of the hull, firmly planting itself in the sand.

With the boat secure, Afam pulled Effia out and into the surf before turning to offer his hand to Awusi. The girl immediately began to splash through the water, dragging her feet and flicking out her legs, launching arcs of spray through the air. The sound of her laughter was a brief tonic to the anxiety that was beginning to take hold in the group now. More men waited for them on the beach, loitering around several blacked-out Mercedes people carriers. To Afam they looked the same as the men they had left at the other side of the water. Sallow, olive skin framed by jet black hair, eyes covered with dark glasses. Guns. Apart from their pirate captain, Afam had seen none of them smile. The men moved down the beach towards them and those who had alighted the boat began to gather around. One of the men carried a large box which he threw onto the sand.

Afam got in line as they put brown paper packages into the hands of each of the refugees. He watched as, one by one, they each peeked inside their bundle and realised what they contained. Documents. Passports. Opportunity.

'What happens now?' Afam asked as he reached the front of the queue.

'That depends...' the man handing out the forgeries pulled a sheet from the envelope he was holding, '... Marco... Whatever is, is not my business any more.' He pushed the package at Afam, who clutched it to his chest. Afam stepped out of the line and dug into the inside pocket of his jacket to retrieve the number he had been given.

'Is there a phone?' he turned back to the man handing out the parcels. The man didn't say anything else, but nodded away across the beach towards a car park where a solitary payphone stood, the dull stainless steel reflecting the sun as a hazy golden orb.

He fingered the scrap of paper as he trudged over the beach, sand piling into the top of his sandals. As he reached the telephone stand he took off his shoes and poured out a seemingly endless stream of sand. He dug into the rear pocket of his trousers, where he had stored the small amount of cash he had, and placed a coin in the slot. He punched in the number and was greeted with an unfamiliar dial tone. After a few moments the call connected.

'*Oui?*' the voice was rough. Afam checked his watch. It was still early — he must have woken the other man. Perhaps he should have waited until later to call.

'*Allo?*' the voice again, more insistent now. Annoyed.

'Hello, sir,' Afam said, not quite sure how to address the stranger, 'My friend gave me this number to call. He said you'd tell me what to do.'

There was a pause, an exaggerated exhalation.

'Oh, Boy Wonder! You made it,' the voice had switched to English now. Afam couldn't work out if he detected a hint of surprise, 'Good, good... do you have a pen?'

Afam hastily scribbled away on the back of the brown envelope they had handed him as the man on the phone laid out the details of how he would have to navigate from the southern coast of Italy to Paris. He had never been on a train before and now what lay before him was another full day of travel, of connections and terminals.

'Don't worry about tickets. These Europeans are so casual with their trains, just walk on. God bless the Schengen visa. If you see the inspector coming, make your way to the bathroom and hide. If you get caught, run. I'll send someone to meet you at Gare du Nord tomorrow morning. Don't be late. Now, lose this number.'

With that, the line disconnected.

10

It had been hard to say goodbye to Awusi and the kids. In the few days they'd spent together, they had grown close, like a family unit. Part of that had been necessity, strength in numbers, but Afam had felt drawn to the young girl, had felt duty bound to ensure that she, her mother and baby brother made it safely across the sea. Perhaps out of some misguided hero complex, perhaps through force of habit — he was used to being expected to step in and look after people. The truth was, despite the expectation, he enjoyed it. Especially after what had happened back home; it felt like a step in the right direction to correcting the balance in the world.

But Afam had different priorities now, the urgency of the new connection lost to the need to find safety and shelter. Awusi planned to stay in southern Italy. There was always work to be found in Puglia — the agricultural centre of the country, cheap labour was always needed and rural Italians were far more likely to not ask questions when it came to official papers.

'Please,' Afam had said, just before they had parted, 'Stay in touch... here...' He tore a scrap of paper from the sheet that held the instructions on travelling to France and scribbled down his email address. 'I've not used it since they made us set one up in school, but I'll check it whenever I can. Send me a note so I know you and the children are safe, have found somewhere to settle.' Awusi promised, and tucked the note into the top of her bra next to the sleeping head of Kojo.

He knelt down to Effia's height and noticed tears in the girl's eyes.

'Be good for your mother,' he said, reaching a hand up to gently wipe away the tears that were forming. 'I will see you all very soon, I promise. I will visit as soon as I'm settled.' Though he meant what he said, Afam had no idea when that would be. How long would he be staying in Paris? How long before he could return home and see his family again? Had him and Leye running away from the scene of the crime implicated them in the death more than anything else ever could? Would he ever be able to get back home to them?

Tears began forming in Afam's eyes again as he contemplated leaving not only his real family, but his temporary family behind. He was alone again, in a new city, a new country, a new continent.

* * *

The Gare du Nord was the biggest building he had ever been inside. He marvelled, wide eyed as he made his way off of the train through the concourse and towards the exit. He noticed that other travellers stayed away from him and understood why as he caught a whiff of his armpit as he moved through the station. It had been days since he had last washed, during which he'd been subjected to extreme desert temperatures and economy train travel that lacked any air conditioning.

He made his way out to the taxi rank outside as he had been instructed, and moved towards a group of men who were huddled, unsmiling, in the shade. No one said anything as he approached, but their gaze switched from the general hubbub of the station specifically towards Afam. He felt intensely uncomfortable as he approached the men.

'How far?' he announced, and three sets of eyebrows raised in surprise before narrowing back into suspicion. 'I'm looking for Isaac?' He framed this as a question. Brows furrowed further, and the men looked at one another. Afam could pick up on the undercurrent of violent tension that emanated from the men. They would usually be people to avoid.

One man stubbed out his cigarette. 'Who's asking?' Afam realised that he hadn't introduced himself.

'I'm Afam...' he waited for acknowledgement in any of the faces but found none, '... from Lagos?'

Still nothing, Afam was beginning to panic as the men now all stood up and moved to close the distance between them.

'What's in the bag?' An unfamiliar voice spoke, deep and chesty, one of the other men broke his silence. He reached out a hand and grasped one of the straps of Afam's rucksack.

Afam's eyes darted around. He seemed to have been backed into a corner, the only way out was to go through the men.

'Sorry,' he tried to keep the quiver out of his voice, 'I think I must have the wrong person.' He clutched his bag to his chest and made to step through the group but they closed ranks making it impossible for him to escape. There were two hands on his rucksack now. Afam's eyes kept darting around, looking for help, looking for an escape. There were people around, but they all seemed to turn away from him whenever he tried to catch their eye.

Another tug at his bag. Afam yanked back, but the hand didn't let go. One of the men, a deep scar tracing his left eye, stepped closer to him. One corner of his mouth raised in a half smile, half sneer.

'Boy Wonder!' Another unfamiliar voice, friendly this time, announced from behind the men, 'You're here. Guys, this one's mine, eh?'

The voice came closer, separating the trio of aggressors, and reaching out to remove their hands from Afam's bag. The man was gigantic, well over six feet and with broad shoulders. Afam could see the definition in his muscles through his t-shirt, which looked a few sizes too small.

'Let's go,' the man said to Afam, nodding away from the dark corner, back towards the street.

'Isaac?' Afam asked.

'And you must be Afam,' the man, Isaac said, 'My car's waiting over there, come on, let's go.'

Afam's experience of cities was confined solely to Lagos. In fairness, it was a city that had everything anyone could ever want. He marvelled as he was driven through the streets of Paris. The Eiffel tower, the Arc d'Triomphe, the ruins of the devastated Notre Dame Cathedral, buildings he had only seen in textbooks at school when he was still a kid, buildings he thought he only ever would see in pictures rose up now from the wide boulevards, surrounded by elaborate, ornate Parisian architecture. People sat outside cafés quietly chatting to one another, or reading newspapers, sipping coffee and eating pastries. He felt a million miles away from the frenetic energy of his home city.

'It's beautiful, no?' Isaac broke the silence, and with it the trance that Afam had found himself in. He had turned around in his seat, paying little attention to the road ahead, in order to talk to Afam. Just like home, Afam thought.

'I've never seen anything like it,' Afam replied.

'I have one more place to show you,' Isaac said, turning back to the road in order to navigate through the crush of cars that swarmed around the tourist hot-spots.

They drove away from the centre of the city for a few minutes, crossing the river, before Isaac spoke up again.

'Here, see,' he said, but Afam was already looking. His head was tucked between the front seats of the car as he looked through the windscreen.

'Parc des Princes?' he asked.

'None other,' Isaac answered, 'Play your cards right at your trial, Boy Wonder, and it won't be long before I'm dropping you off here for training!'

Afam didn't say anything, just stared up at the ramparts of the colossal building. It was a fortress that stretched up into the desolate sky, clouds hanging heavy overhead. At regular intervals, scimitars of concrete sliced out of the walls. It was as magnificent as it was intimidating. You could see how the home team and fans would be made to feel safe within the citadel whilst visitors would feel particularly unwelcome.

They drove past the stadium and carried on a little way down a multi-lane road before Isaac pulled off. The buildings they found here had none of the glamour of the city they'd just been through. They were far and above anything that Afam had seen up close before, but paled in comparison to the grandiosity they'd found in central Paris.

'Where are we?' Afam asked.

'Just need to pick someone up,' Isaac said, this time not looking back.

Afam's brow furrowed at his host's sudden reticence.

'So, how long before I get to go to my trial?' he asked. Actually arriving in Paris had made him hopeful. He hadn't thought twice about the false pretences they had brought here him on, the club trial that everyone had convinced him was fake, but now he was back on terra firma, it felt achievable. 'Will I have somewhere to stay? I have some money, so I could find a hotel?' Afam tried again, but his string of questions was met with silence as Isaac navigated through street after street. It looked identical to him: high-rise apartment blocks set apart from one another by dirty shopfronts. On one, the stainless steel shutters had been torn open on one side giving the building a lopsided grin. The window behind was smashed through. Someone had sprayed graffiti across the facade, though Afam couldn't understand what it said. Nothing good.

They turned a corner off of the high street and pulled up alongside a group of men who were loitering around a bench smoking cigarettes and sipping from a bottle of brandy. Isaac sounded the horn and a giant mastiff with bite marks on its ears and a scowl made permanent by a scar on its top lip looked up as the car approached, its eyes fixed, ears pinned back until one of the men yanked on the chain that attached it to the bench. The animal gave up its watch and lay its head down on its paws.

Two of the men approached the car, flanking it on either side, and opened the rear doors. One of the men was wider than he was tall, and seemed to heave his whole body forward with every step, dabbing at his forehead with a handkerchief he kept balled in a meaty fist. The other man was almost the exact opposite of his companion. Rake thin, his long legs looked as though they could barely hold his weight, his arms draped inside the front pocket of his hoody. He had pulled the hood up over his head and the drawstring was pulled tight so that only his nose, his lips and his eyes could be seen.

Afam shifted into the centre seat as the men got into the car wordlessly, expecting whatever was in their way to just move. On instinct, Afam drew his bag to his chest. He said nothing as the men greeted Isaac, sharing handshakes and high-fives, catching up on various pieces of gossip. They began driving again, still neither man introduced themselves to Afam, and Isaac had lost the sheen he had once had of the accommodating host. He hadn't spoken a word to him since they had left the PSG stadium.

'Hi,' Afam tried to break the ice, 'How do you guys know Isaac?'

'If I told you that, I'd have to kill you,' said the man to Afam's left. Afam let out an awkward laugh, which was cut short by a heavy metal clunk. Afam knew the sound. It was unmistakable. He had seen plenty of guns before. Some all too recently. The first time he'd seen one was when Leye's cousin had brought one to show off amongst the smaller kids at the pitch. He felt an uncomfortable jab in his ribs and turned towards the skinny man.

Afam's eyes widened as he looked down and saw the man holding a handgun against his kidneys.

'Bag,' he said, he'd taken his hood off now and Afam saw a livid scar running down the right side of his face onto his neck. It wasn't the first scar he'd seen today and made Afam wonder whether the two were linked.

Afam didn't fight as the larger man snatched the bag from his grip and began rifling through. He pulled out the sheaf of documents that Afam had hidden at the bottom beneath his clothes and tucked it into his jacket.

'Hey!' Afam couldn't help himself. He had been through hell to get those papers, to escape what he'd done back home. They were his chance at freedom, not just from escaping implication in Samuel's accident, but in starting a new life, supporting his family.

'Relax,' the skinny man said, in a tone that didn't do anything to calm Afam's nerves, 'You'll get it back. You didn't think it was free, though, did you? Gotta work for this, brother.'

'I will. As soon as I get through my trial, I'll pay you double what it's worth. I promise. Just give it back. Please.'

Everyone in the car burst into laughter.

'Isaac, you hear this? What bullshit did you string him on this time?'

Afam saw Isaac shake his head in the rear-view mirror, wiping a tear away from his eye.

'Come on man, out,' the fat man finally spoke. The car slowed, and skinny got out, scanning the streets briefly before ushering

Afam out with the gun. Afam didn't need to be told again and scrambled across the seat through the open door. He felt a thud on his back as the fat man threw his bag out of the car after him. The crew erupted into another fit of hysterics.

'Don't go far now, hear me?' the skinny man said as he reentered the car. He closed the door and rolled down the window, the barrel of the gun pointing at Afam the entire time, 'We'll find you. Tell you what we need you to do.'

With that, the car shifted into gear and sped off down the street, tyres screeching against the tarmac.

Afam watched it speed off and lost sight of it as it turned a corner up ahead. He stooped to pick up his bag, piling his possessions back in where they had spilled on the pavement. He stood for a moment, closed his eyes as if in deep thought, and took a deep breath, letting it out very slowly. Reaching for the strap, he slung his bag over his shoulder and headed back the way they had come, back towards the city.

11

Afam needed to find water. He had been walking for hours. When he had found himself ousted from Isaac's car, his bag a little lighter than before, he had set off back the way they had come, looking for the river they had crossed. The Seine, he remembered. He didn't know what he was going to do when he found it, but knew that eventually it would lead him back to the city, to the Paris from his schoolbooks. After a while he realised that despite traipsing the promenade that ran along the bank, he didn't recognise anything they had driven past. He walked for miles, the morning sun warming as it reached its high point at midday; with every step his feet, and his heart, became a little heavier.

Eventually he came across a bridge and a nearby sign suggested crossing it would lead him to the city again. Afam decided that he would make his way to the Parc des Princes, the stadium at which PSG played their home games, and explain the situation there. He wasn't stupid, he knew now what he'd suspected all along, that the promises of European football trials were just lies. Lies told to lure young people away from their homes, to abandon them in strange cities and force them to do their bidding in order for a ticket home. Afam thought about Awusi, about Effia. Their story would be a different one than his. Afam could work, he could put himself to good use doing a multitude of things. He didn't doubt that Awusi was similarly well skilled — when you were as poor as they were, you had to be adaptable — but he also knew what happened to young women in the hands of criminals.

Afam closed his eyes and prayed that they would be okay. He would get in touch with them as soon as he figured out what he was doing here. He refused to give in to the people who had brought him here. They had abandoned him, but now he had anonymity on his side — they had no way of finding him. It was up to him now to make his way here.

'Excuse me,' Afam spoke English to a passerby who kept her eyes glued to the phone as she breezed past him, oblivious to the fact she'd been spoken to. Afam couldn't believe it, he had never encountered such a thing. Back home it felt like you could stop anyone in the street for directions and before you knew it you'd have been chatting for half an hour, setting the world to rights. He carried on, scanning his fellow pedestrians for a friendly face.

He approached a group of people, adults and children, stopped on a street corner. They wore matching bright red baseball caps and the adults — he presumed them to be the parents of the kids — wore garish bags around their waists. Afam walked up to them sheepishly, trying to catch the father's eyes as he approached. A hush descended amongst the group, the mother wrapping an arm around each of her children who had stopped whatever game they had been playing amongst themselves. People went rigid, their eyes wide as they assessed the stranger approaching them.

'Hi,' Afam said, putting on the most genial smile he could muster. He noticed a slight relaxation amongst the group as they recognised English. Afam closed the gap and continued, 'I need some help, please...' the adults tensed again as they played out an awkward situation with a beggar in their heads. Sensing their change in mood, Afam pressed on as quickly as he could, 'I'm a little lost. I'm supposed to be meeting a friend but they haven't shown up.'

'You and me both, buddy!' the father blasted out in an American accent; Afam didn't know enough about the country to say exactly where in America it was from. 'My phone's out of battery and I left the charger back at the hotel. Only problem is... we don't know how to get back there! And it's true what they say about these Parisians, y'know. So rude! We've been trying to get people to help us but no one's stopped yet.'

'I don't know what the fuss is all about, Paris ain't that great a country so far,' the man's wife chimed in.

'Say, where are you from — you don't sound local,' the man continued.

'Lagos,' Afam replied.

'Lagos... that's Africa right? I've heard it's a great place. Maybe we'll go there next summer — are the people as rude as they are here?'

Afam shrugged, 'Some of them, I suppose.'

'Daddy, I want to get out of here — let's just find a Starbucks?' the girl interrupted.

'Okay, hun,' the father rolled his eyes as he looked at Afam, 'Hey buddy, sorry we couldn't help. Good luck, okay?'

'See you in Lagos,' Afam smiled and watched the family walk off, looking the wrong way as they crossed the road. A moped slammed on its brakes and blared its horn as they walked straight out in front of it.

'Hey buddy, watch where you're going!' Afam heard the father yell as he shepherded his family across the road.

'*Excusez-moi,*' Afam heard someone speak behind him and turned towards the voice. 'You need some help?'

Afam's grinned broadly, relief etched across his face. He nodded. A young woman stood behind him. Afam had never seen someone dressed so strangely. She was dressed from head to toe in black.

Torn stockings were matched by a short leather skirt, black denim jacket adorned with various indecipherable cotton patches. She wore heavy biker boots and had painted her face with thick, alabaster make up and rimmed her lips and eyes with a kohl pencil. Her hair continued the monochrome theme; parted down the middle, she had bleached one side white, dyed the other jet black.

'Where are you looking for?'

'Um,' Afam still couldn't quite believe what he was looking at. She looked like a witch. But witch or no witch, she was his only help, 'I'm looking for the stadium. Football.' He could barely get the words out.

'Oh, that's easy,' the girl smiled, revealing a row of perfect white teeth, a metal ring with a jewel clasp hanging between the middle top teeth. Afam listened intently, trying not to get too distracted as he counted the piercings on the girl's face and ears. She tore a piece of paper from a pad that she had in her rucksack — black as well, with a large anarchist A scratched onto it in white-out — and drew him a simple map showing directions to the stadium. Afam couldn't believe his luck.

'Thank you so much!' he effused, 'I can't tell you how important this is.' The girl smiled. 'Hey, what's your name?'

'Sophie,' the girl smiled again, one of the warmest smiles Afam had ever seen.

'Sophie, I owe you. A lot. Can you give me your email — one day, soon, I'll be able to repay you.'

'It's okay, *pas de probleme*,' Sophie said, and folded up the sheet of paper and handed it to Afam.

'Please?'

Sophie shrugged, wrote down an address on the back of the folded map and handed it to Afam.

'Thank you, so much,' Afam said, 'I promise you, I'll pay you back one day.'

'*Au revoir*,' Sophie said, and turned to head over the bridge, the same way Afam had come from.

* * *

Afam had followed Sophie's map to the letter and even though he had only driven past the PSG stadium at a distance, he didn't recognise anything around him. It didn't help that all the streets seemed to look the same here. Same buildings, same road signs, same people.

He was now on the final street on the hand-drawn map but couldn't see anything quite as impressive as the building he'd seen before. There were a few small shops and a quiet bar, the bistro tables outside empty but for one solitary, sultry man. Afam watched as the man took a cigarette out of a packet in his shirt pocket and used the one he'd just been smoking to light it. He took a deep drag, closed his eyes and exhaled through his nose.

Afam slumped down at the table next to the man and leaned forwards, his head in his hands. Something had gone wrong. Everything had gone wrong. All he wanted to do was go back home, to sit with his sister and brothers on their front porch as Iman read and the boys ...

The man finished his cigarette, stubbing it out in the heavy ceramic ashtray. He got up, wiped his hands across the front of his shirt, flicking off ash. The buttons strained to hold in his stomach as he pulled his shoulders back, stretched both arms into the air and shook his whole body before a hacking cough erupted from his lungs. He walked straight past Afam into the bar behind, the door hinges offering a plaintive squeal as though it had been far too long since any patrons had stepped foot inside.

Afam sat up and slouched in his chair. The sun had passed its peak and was casting long shadows as it moved West, sinking towards the horizon. He would have to find somewhere to sleep, soon. Food could wait, but he still needed water. He grabbed his rucksack and made to head inside, hoping that whoever ran the place would let him use the bathroom. He could drink from the tap. As he stood up, the smoking man emerged from the bar, tray in hand, a small glass filled with beer and a bowl of peanuts.

'*Voila*,' the man said, setting the tray down on the table.

'Please, no, I cannot pay,' he said, embarrassed at the admission. The man paused, looked at the drink and snack he'd put down, looked at Afam and delivered a shrug so exaggerated that his shoulders grazed his ears. He smiled at Afam, held up one finger, imploring him to wait, and returned through the creaky door. Moments later, he returned, his own glass filled to the brim with amber ale and resumed his seat.

'*Sante*,' he said, raising his glass. Afam followed suit, reaching out to clink the beer with his new friend. He took a deep sip, the coolness of the beer reviving him, and it took all of his willpower not to gulp down the entire glass.

'Phillipe,' the man introduced himself, smirking as he looked at Afam's half-empty glass.

'Afam,' he said, grabbing a handful of the peanuts and shoving them all in his mouth. He couldn't remember the last time he'd eaten. The kebab at the port had been his last square meal.

'So... um... why are you here? I'm sorry, my English is not good. How did you get here?'

With that, the floodgates opened. Whilst he didn't let Phillipe know why he'd had to leave Lagos, he detailed the entire journey, the sea crossing, the travel through Italy to France, and then Isaac and his friends. At the back of his mind, he knew it was dangerous to be quite so open — he had heard that Europeans didn't take kindly to illegal immigrants. But Phillipe sat and listened, quietly sipping his beer, his eyes wide as he heard Afam's extraordinary struggle.

'And now you're here. St Ouen. Why? It's a small place. People usually end up in the city.'

'Well,' Afam started, 'They promised me a trial. These guys. I guess that was all just a lie, but anyway, I thought that if I could just get to the stadium, I could talk to someone at PSG and... well, I don't really know...'

'What? You thought you'd just walk into the lobby, tell them 'I'm here to play', and they'd let you in? *Merde*, you're crazy, man, crazy!' Phillippe burst out laughing 'But anyway, you are very far from Parc des Princes - you went the long way round!'

'A girl helped me, she drew me a map,' Afam was laughing with Phillipe now, his desperation giving way to a sort of manic laughter at everything.

'Ah! Look at this!' Phillipe snatched the scrap of paper away from him, 'Ha! Oh man, she wasn't so wrong after all. She directed you to the stadium... just, not the one you wanted to get to!'

'What do you mean?'

'Look, man, over there,' Phillipe pointed across the road.

Afam couldn't believe he hadn't noticed before. Directly opposite the bar a small sign announced Stade. Floodlights towered over the four corners of the low stands, and Afam gazed across the car park to the ticket booths and turnstiles at the front of the building.

'What's this?' he asked Phillipe.

'The true Paris football club,' came the answer, with a pride reserved for supporters of lower-league football teams.

'They're lower league?' Excitement rose in Afam's chest as Phillipe nodded. He slid his bag over to his feet and unzipped it, checking through his possessions. The boots that Samuel had given him were still there. 'I need to go,' he said to Phillipe, and stood up, slinging his bag over his shoulder. 'I will pay you for the drink, one day, I swear — I just need to do this.'

'Of course, Afam. I'll put it on your tab,' Phillipe said, though smiled in a way that reassured Afam his debt was already repaid.

Afam headed across the road, cutting behind a car that drove past the bar. He crossed the car park quickly and headed for the turnstiles. The shutters on the ticket office were closed, the place looked dead, though he could hear activity coming from inside. He went left, skirting the perimeter of the stadium until he found a side entrance with a reception lobby. Taking a deep breath, he walked through the automatic doors into the air-conditioned lobby and took a moment to relish the coolness of the room as opposed to the blazing heat of the sun outside. A man sat behind the front desk, a telephone receiver pressed to his ear. He raised a hand as Afam approached and continued his conversation and then gestured to a set of low-slung leather armchairs situated around a glass and chrome coffee table. Newspapers and magazines were artfully arranged on the table and Afam took a seat and began leafing through the collection, trying to make sense of the French.

After several minutes, the man behind the desk approached Afam. He was not much taller standing than he'd been sitting down and Afam felt uncomfortable as he rose to greet him. Afam offered his hand, which the man looked at and ignored, as he began asking what Afam presumed to be questions. Upon receiving a series of blank looks, the man switched to English.

'What. Are. You. Doing. Here?' he asked, speaking slowly, his tone frustrated and condescending.

'I'm here for a trial,' Afam replied.

The man scoffed. 'Who are you meeting with?' he asked.

'I can't remember his name. My agent told me to come here.' It shocked Afam, how easily the lie was forming. The man rolled his eyes, turned and walked back to his desk, picking up the telephone again. Afam watched as the man spoke into the handset in hushed tones. Even if Afam were able to make out the language, the man was deliberately speaking in whispers. He looked up at Afam as he spoke, smiled, and returned to his conversation. He placed the receiver back on its cradle and called out to Afam.

'Someone will be down for you soon,' he said.

Afam couldn't believe his luck. He had chanced his arm and things were now in motion. This could be his big break. His heart beat faster so he sat back and continued leafing through the magazines, trying to bring his nerves under control. He jumped at a commotion of loud voices and laughter emerging into the lobby and looked up to see several people he assumed were players making their way through the building, laughing and joking as they carried kit bags.

As he gazed at the men, he didn't notice another man approaching his position at the table. The man wore an ill-fitting polyester suit, his tie was clip-on, and he carried a walkie-talkie in one hand that crackled with indecipherable noise. Afam turned as the man pressed a button on the side of his handset and spoke into it in rapid-fire French.

'Sir,' the security guard spoke to Afam, his tone firm, heavily accented, 'It's time to leave.'

'But—' Afam objected, 'I have a trial here today.'

'Sir, there are no trials here today. We appreciate your interest and hope to see you in the stands soon,' the guard said in a well-practised tone: gentle but firm, enough to encourage you to do exactly what he told you to, but to feel as though it was your idea in the first place.

'But my agent told me... honestly, look, I was scouted from my township in Lagos — I've come a very long way for this' Afam was desperate, he could feel the opportunity slipping through his fingers. 'Hey, don't touch my bag,' he snatched the holdall back from the guard and hugged it close. 'Please,' he added.

Hearing the fracas, two of the men from the group of footballers moved over to investigate.

'Hey,' one said, 'What's going on?'

'Nothing to see here, sir. This young man says he's here for a trial, but there's nothing marked in the calendar. Just a chancer,' the man sneered.

The footballer smirked and turned to look at his teammates.

'You're that good, eh? Think you can just rock up here and play?' he said to Afam, 'Where you from?'

'Lagos,' Afam blurted, shaking his arm free of the grip of the security guard.

The footballer hesitated, 'Where about?'

'AJ City,' Afam said.

The man's eyes widened in surprise.

'No way! We're like neighbours — I'm from Festac Town! Hey, what's your name?'

'Afam,' he said, and then, 'I'm sorry, I don't recognise you.'

'You wouldn't,' shot one of the men's teammates and they all burst into laughter.

'Ignore them, Afam — I'm Victor. So, you really think you could get a trial here? You that good?'

'I'm good,' Afam said, adrenaline coursing through him. He had to think fast, he couldn't afford one wrong move. It could cost him his chance. Could cost a lot more.

Victor signalled for the guard to release Afam's arm, which he reluctantly did. Afam rubbed at where the guard had held him and looked around for his bag.

'You reckon you can hack it in the big leagues, then?' he asked, raising an eyebrow, tilting his head upwards to appraise Afam.

'There's only one way to find out,' Afam retorted, pushing back against the challenge.

'Come on then,' Victor said. He turned to his teammates, 'Boys, come on — let's give Afam his big break.' The other men looked at each other, shrugged, and followed Victor who had already begun making his way back down the corridor to what Afam assumed would be the pitch.

* * *

'Afam, I don't know who you are, or where you came from, but I want to see if there's something we can do for you.'

Afam sat with a man who had introduced himself as Moussa, the youth team coach. He had been off of the pitch for a while now, but his heart still raced, the palms of his hands felt sweaty, and he became painfully aware of the hole in the front of his shirt. He had thrown everything he had at his mock-try out and very soon Victor and his friends had stopped laughing as Afam ran rings around them. Gradually, staff members had come over to watch as the random kid off the street twisted and turned around some of their B-Team squad and when the 3-a-side game finished a soft ripple of applause went round the sideline.

As he walked off the pitch, Moussa had been waiting. Victor had made the introduction and Moussa had taken Afam into a small room at the side of the pitch. The room was sterile, with a projector screen at one end and a wall of glass at the other. A table was situated in the centre of the room, surrounded by several high-end desk chairs emblazoned with the team's logo. They had sat for a while, talking about football, about the weather, cars, girls. When it came to questions about where Afam had come from, though, he had clammed up. He had explained certain parts of his situation: that he had left his village in search of football stardom, that the men who had bought him here had promised him a trial at PSG, that those men had robbed him.

Moussa had sensed this was not an area in which to press the boy and had deftly moved the conversation on to talk about their youth outreach program.

'You've walked the streets here, you've seen what it's like?' Moussa said, 'I mean, it's not quite Beirut, but there's not a lot of money here. A lot of people out of work. A lot of immigrants in work, but being paid peanuts.' Afam nodded along as Moussa spoke. 'Our history is in our community, a lot of players came through this team and went on to do great things. Lots of kids went through the academy and then onto top flight teams. Some even got a few caps. Anyway, the point I'm trying to make is that from what I saw today, we'd like to get you back here for a proper trial, not just some kick-about. Where are you staying?'

'I...' Afam cringed, 'I'm staying in a hotel somewhere near the city.' He hated the lie.

'That narrows it down a bit,' Moussa laughed, 'Look, how long were you planning on staying on here?'

'I don't know.' Afam couldn't believe how easily the lies rolled off of his tongue, 'I don't really have any plans. I was thinking about finding a place once I'd found some work.'

'How about this? A few of the guys in our reserve squad have a spare room at their apartment, not too far from here — a little closer to the city. Let me call them and see if we can put you up there just for the meantime, while we get your trial sorted. I'm guessing that you don't have a lot of money on you given those men robbed you?' Afam shook his head, averted his eyes.

'No sweat, it will all be fine,' Moussa continued. He dug into his pocket and pulled out his wallet. He extracted a card and passed it to Afam. 'Take this. Go to any corner store and get yourself a cheap handset and a SIM. Take my number,' Moussa handed over his business card, 'And call me as soon as you do. I'll speak to the boys about the spare room. Like I say, it'll be all good. Once that's all sorted, we can start thinking about giving you a run-out in front of the big bosses and all that stuff.'

Afam felt steamrollered. He didn't quite know what had just happened, but before he could begin to protest, Moussa's phone rang. He checked the screen, his eyes rolled, and he looked up at Afam.

'Sorry, have to take this. Speak to you soon. Don't spend all my money,' he said, got up and walked towards the door, already talking to whoever was at the end of the line.

12

Annabel raised her coffee cup to her lips and found it empty. More coffee needed.

She had, as ever, packed her emergency travel coffee kit — a plastic Hario V60 pour-over device that sat on top of your mug, paper filters, and a ceramic burr hand grinder. Despite the cafe culture in Paris, and France being the birthplace of the ubiquitous cafetiere, French coffee never impressed Annabel. A cafetiere was made for sharing — brew a full pot to yourself and you ended up with one fair to middling cup and the rest turning to bitter, over extracted sludge as it continued to steep in the pot. It got the job done, but life was too short for bad coffee, she reasoned and so had gone to one of the new wave of Parisian coffee shops that fitted the model of the Antipodean coffee boom that had swept London, with cortados and flat whites, non-dairy milks, vegan sausage rolls and *pastel de nata*. She had bought a bag of single-origin Ethiopian beans and went back to her hotel room to spend time with the megabytes of information Chloé had given her.

Sifting through emails was one of the worst parts of the job. Normally she would have a few people helping her, but given the nature of what she was trying to find she didn't want to get anyone else involved yet. Any sort of leaking could force people to go to ground and destroy evidence, which would make the whole endeavour pointless. And so, she scrolled. She had worked up a system whereby she deleted anything irrelevant — there was a lot of that — and then prioritised communications into folders according to how pertinent they seemed to what she was trying to discover: evidence of Georges Pepin taking bribes from fake African academies, but also any unusual communications from the sports ministry, or indeed from any questionable outside contacts. She had already found several things that could prove useful. Perhaps counter-intuitively it was always the emails with the least information that proved most interesting. Simple missives with dates and times, with phone numbers, all pointed towards someone holding something back, something they didn't want to have traced back to them.

Coffee brewed, Annabel sat back down on her bed and pulled the covers over her feet, placing her computer on her lap. She sipped the coffee and started poring through the messages again but after a while was finding it hard to maintain her concentration. Food, then. The caffeine wasn't having its full effect as an appetite suppressant. She opened up two new tabs on her laptop; her messenger service and Google Maps. She clicked the 'Restaurants' icon at the top of the maps page and then flicked back to the Signal app. It was her preferred end-to-end encryption service: she trusted anything designed to stop governments spying on private citizens a lot more than she did the Facebook-owned messaging software used by most people, and had made sure Chloé downloaded it to her phone for any future communications. As it happened, she had received a message from Chloé:

Have a name for you, from Robert: Thierry Leger. Also, you should talk to Diouf.

Annabel didn't recognise the name, but pasted it into the search bar in the folder containing the emails hoping a deep search would flag something pertinent. She checked the maps tab to see if it had thrown up anywhere for her to eat — she didn't want to order another day-old croque monsieur from room service — but as she expected, all that was recommended was a long list of classic Parisian bistros. Tourist traps. She fired back a message to Chloé:

Great, thanks! You mean Emmanuel Diouf? The player? Hey, quick q: anywhere good to eat round here?

She tossed her phone onto her bed and got up to pull on her coat and shoes. A minute or two later, she heard her phone buzz. Chloe had come good with a list of local eateries as well as confirming that the Diouf she referred to was indeed Emmanuel Diouf. He was something of a hero on the terraces and had had a few run outs for the national side. Annabel had recently done a profile piece on him, she was sure she had his contact details. It was interesting, Annabel thought Diouf had been incredibly honest and open, but he hadn't mentioned anything about any untoward practices regarding his arrival in France. Clearly her bullshit radar needed a bit of fine tuning. She opened up the email app on her phone and fired off a quick email to Diouf's agent, saying she needed some follow-up information for the piece that hadn't run yet. She saw that she'd received an email. The address was a randomly assigned 'burner' mail, designed to be untraceable. She opened the message. There was no body text, but there were several PDF attachments. It didn't take Annabel long to figure out what she was looking at. The files were copies of Emmanuel Diouf's banking statements; money in and money out. She cast a quick eye over the list and noticed that the anonymous sender had highlighted certain transactions. Huge amounts of money going out of the account to an organisation called Share the Love. Was Diouf's story about his journey to France a fabrication? Could his trial have been genuine, which is how he started his career, but his origin story false? He had told her his manager was a close family friend who had stuck by them for years. But what if that was a lie? What if his manager was some sort of enforcer, and Share the Love was a front for sending a cut of his earnings back to the gangsters who had made him? She closed the email, grabbed her bag from the bathroom counter, took her keycard from the slot by the door and headed out.

* * *

'Ms. Green?' a voice called out to Annabel as she made her way through the hotel lobby. She turned towards the source of the noise.

'Hello?' she didn't recognise the man. He was 'official' looking, well-dressed in an expensive, off-the-rack suit. She couldn't help but dress people down, a habit born from having a tailor as a grandfather. The man got up from his seat in the corner of the lobby, placing the magazine he had been reading on the coffee table.

'Hi,' he closed the gap, 'Don't worry, I come in peace.' He held out his hands in front of him, palms towards Annabel. An ancient form to show he wasn't carrying a weapon, it didn't set Annabel's mind at ease. No one knew she was in the country. How had this man found her? How had he found where she was staying?

'I think we have a mutual friend in Ms. Martin? I saw you meeting with her at our offices a few days ago. Quite an animated conversation.' His English was perfect, though inflected with a heavy French accent.

Annabel couldn't see the value in lying — the man had clearly seen her with Chloé. She would need to play things close, though — she still wasn't sure what his intentions were.

'Yes, she does get a little overexcited when talking about her work.' Annabel instantly realised her mistake.

'Tell me,' the man asked, picking up on the misstep, 'what aspects of her work is it you're interested in? If you don't mind my asking?'

'Sorry, but who are you again? You don't have any business knowing about the content of a private conversation between two grown women.' Annabel was on the defensive and she knew it. She couldn't let this guy get the better of her. Who was he? Why was he asking questions about Chloé? It wasn't Georges Pepin, Annabel had done an internet deep dive on him as soon as she had got back to her hotel room. It never failed to surprise her how much information people put about themselves on the internet. Within minutes of her first click, Annabel had Pepin's school and work history, LinkedIn blog posts and Instagram feed. His blog posts were par for the course: self-aggrandising humble-brags detailing the charity work he did, business 'insights' and the cod-philosophical musings of someone who'd only read the headlines. His Instagram feed was a string of top-down photos of brunch, in-flight photos of aeroplane wings and assorted shots with family and friends. Annabel had spent some time seeing whether it was possible to glean any information from the metadata on the photos, thinking it might add grist to the mill, but any EXIF data was stripped from the files.

'As I said, Ms Green, I am a colleague of Ms. Martin. My name is Félix. I work on a separate project to Chloé, but there is sufficient crossover that it has become a matter of interest that she may be talking to a British journalist of such repute.'

There was a tinge of threat in Félix's voice that made Annabel prick up.

'I'm doing a story about a French youth academy at a lower-league team. Chloé was letting me know about how they link up with clubs in Africa. You know, what she does for a living.' Annabel fired back, matching Félix's aggression.

'Ah, yes, of course — the real heart of Parisian football. Salt of the earth. How is Moussa? Such a shame about that knee — he could have really been someone.'

'Football's loss is humanity's gain,' said Annabel, her hackles raised at the slight on her good friend, 'Listen, Félix, I don't know who you are, or what you're insinuating, but the conversation I had with Chloé was all on the level. But it was private, and as a matter of principle I'm not going to tell you a single word that was uttered. You have no right to know. I do not know you, and frankly, nor do I have any desire to get to know you. Now, unless you have anything more to add, I'm on my way out.'

Félix smiled a Cheshire-cat grin.

'Ms. Green, I'm sorry to have taken your time. It's just that I wanted to reach out to you and suggest that you might be better off looking elsewhere. Ms. Martin has some... peculiar ideas about goings-on at our organisation, and I want to assure you that they're little more than conspiratorial ramblings. Ms. Martin is a valued member of our team, but she can so often get caught up in her own ideas. I'm sure you understand that what someone thinks they see is not always the objective reality?'

'Thanks for the tip,' Annabel shot back, 'Now, if you don't mind?' she indicated towards the main entrance.

'Of course,' Félix said, 'I merely wanted to warn you against the damage that being associated with such a wild card might do to your career.'

'Is that a threat?' Annabel bristled.

'Of course not, Ms. Green — just some friendly advice. It would be a shame to see such a prominent journalist as yourself fall flat on her face in public. The work you do is so important. Speaking truth to power, isn't that what you do? Where would we be without you? Anyway, I won't keep you a moment longer... enjoy your lunch.'

With that, Annabel moved swiftly towards the exit. As she reached the doors, she fished in her bag for an umbrella. It was raining again.

13

No matter how many times Annabel found herself within the inner sanctums of top-flight players, she never failed to be impressed by the splendour. A brief, dark, thought crossed her mind that her reaction was the same as countless women, and she could see how easily one could be swept up in the glamour, brought back to someone's glitzy pad and encouraged to do things you otherwise wouldn't dream of.

The taxi had driven through the gates, which had opened remotely, and up the gravel driveway towards Diouf's property. The private drive led to a courtyard in front of the house. Several cars sat neatly in a row — a top of the line Range Rover Evoque that had had a tasteful Overfinch customisation shared the space with a sports car slung so low to the ground that Annabel doubted it had even the clearance to deal with a garage forecourt, and a more austere Tesla Model X that Annabel guessed served as the family car. She couldn't see a car seat fitting in the bucket seats in the Lamborghini.

Emmanuel was waiting for her at the door, which was wide open, revealing a vast, open-plan bottom floor. A spacious living area spanned out in front of her with a sofa that looked as though it could seat an entire football team including reserves and the coaching squad. At the back of the room, floor to ceiling windows opened out onto what looked like at least an acre of garden. A pool and jacuzzi were gently lit in the early evening light by spotlights set into the deck, and Annabel spied an outdoor dining area complete with wood-fired pizza oven and stainless steel kitchen set up. The dinner parties must have been remarkable, Annabel thought, spying the wine-fridges.

'Annabel, good to see you again,' Emmanuel welcomed her, 'I hope you don't mind coming out to me — I've only just come back from the city, and I'm supposed to be resting. I couldn't bear the thought of more Paris traffic so soon.'

'Not at all,' said Annabel, trying to imagine the person who would be annoyed to be invited into such luxury.

'Take a seat, please. Can I get you a drink or something? I'm having a beer, if you want?'

'I could murder a beer,' Annabel said, remembering what she had told Moussa about journalists and their reputation for alcohol.

Annabel seated herself on the sofa and took out her jotter and pen, the analogue tools of the trade that continued to serve her well. Dictaphones, iPhone, laptops all served their purpose most of the time, but there was something more intimate, more disarming about a pen and paper. And Annabel had spent a lot of effort learning shorthand that she didn't want to waste.

Emmanuel returned a few moments later with a couple of bottles of lager and handed one to Annabel, then chinked the neck of his to her bottle.

'Santé.'

'*L'chaim,*' Annabel replied, unsure of why she'd dredged up the Hebrew phrase, a distant memory of family celebrations from her childhood.

They each took deep swigs from the bottles and paused for a moment, feeling the loosening effects of the first alcohol. It was Emmanuel who broke the silence.

'So, my manager tells me you had a few follow-up questions?'

'Yes,' Annabel re-centered her attention on the job at hand, 'It was just a few things my editor wanted to clear up before we run the piece. I saw the pics the photographer did — they're great. I loved the ones with you and the kids, and your wife. You look like a happy family.'

'We are!' Emmanuel answered without pause, 'When you've come from where I started, of course you love all the things that money brings, but it's the little things that really matter. I know they say that money can't buy you happiness, but I grew up not knowing where the next meal was coming from, my kids never have to worry about that.'

'Money can buy you happiness,' Annabel added, 'But it's not the stuff you can buy that brings that happiness. It's the comfort, the security, isn't it?'

'Exactly, and that's why I do so much still with people at home. I tried to buy my parents a big house back home, but they wouldn't have it. I mean, they got a bigger house, but it's not a mansion. They've stayed close to the community, and they've helped me identify areas where I could put my money to good use. They run Share the Love for me. I'm not interested in giving money to a corporation who sorts out its board before taking any action. My money is for direct action. It puts food on tables, gets clean drinking water into every home. I don't want this piece to sound like a big PR stunt for me, Annabel; some big 'oh, look at me, look how much I give to other people' puff piece. That's not what it's about. I suppose it's about getting others who are in my position to think about what they do with their money. To make sure people don't forget their roots. Football is like no other sport in the world that it can, and does, pull people out of poverty. There's no school you have to get into in order to meet the right people, it doesn't matter who your parents are, you just have to be good at football. It's the peoples' game, played by the people. No one needs as much money as I have, and I'm nowhere near the richest footballer, nowhere near. But it's hard to get people to do good with their money. There can be this sense of 'well I worked hard for it, why does anyone else deserve it?' which I get, but it makes for a sad world when we lose our community spirit — when we stop giving back.'

'I couldn't agree more,' Annabel said, her journalist nose catching the whiff of Share the Love, 'and I think you'll be pleased when you see the piece. I'll make sure you see it before we run it.' She paused a moment, building up the courage to broach a difficult topic.

'Emmanuel, what I actually wanted to talk to you about was the bit in your story about how you came from Senegal to Paris. I've been talking to a few people who work with kids coming out of Africa and, frankly, am hearing some complete horror stories. You've got these legit academies who work with the European leagues to scout the best talent and arrange their trials, travel, bed and board, but then I'm also hearing some stories about shady practices, where fake academies are set up in order, essentially, to rob the families of these promising kids. The families are told to stump up cash, their kids are set up with 'managers' who create the itinerary, but then when the kids reach Paris they're abandoned. The managers run off with the cash and they leave the kids to fend for themselves. Is that something you've come across?'

Emmanuel shifted in his seat, casting his eyes around the room as he tried to avoid eye contact with Annabel. He took a long sip of his beer, opened his mouth to say something, but then thought better of it and returned the bottle to his lips. Time seemed to stretch out between them before Emmanuel finally came back round to her.

'No,' he said, bluntly. 'I mean, I've heard the stories, but no one I know has ever mentioned that.'

Annabel considered Emmanuel's answer, alongside his awkward body language and pressed on.

'Or what about people smugglers? Such a romantic name, sorry — human traffickers? One of my contacts was telling me that as much as these fake academies are being set up, with dubious moral practices, there's also a problem with gangs. European branches of African criminal gangs — like the Area Boys in Nigeria, or the Senegalese mafia — who continue to turn the screws on the kids once they're here. I've seen records of your donations and there's an extraordinary amount of money flowing back into Senegal. It would be easy to make assumptions that some of that money was being funnelled into the wrong channels.' Annabel was trying to give Emmanuel an opening to talk, to hint that she suspected the story he'd told her before about coming to France wasn't quite the whole truth.

'Are you saying I'm a gangster?' Emmanuel tried to make it sound like he was joking, but there was something behind what he said. He fixed Annabel with a hard stare. 'I already told you last time. I came here with Ousman. He's still my manager after all these years. He didn't rip me off, he's not a gangster. He's a good man who has stuck with my family and me all of these years.'

'I'm not talking about Ousman, no. Sorry, I didn't mean to offend. I just wondered whether you'd heard these stories, what that meant for you and for the work Share the Love is doing.' Annabel backtracked slightly, not wanting to shut down the line of enquiry at the outset.

'Of course I've heard the stories,' it didn't seem to Annabel as though Emmanuel was calming down. He was on the defensive, but also seemed unsettled in another way, as though he was afraid of someone hearing what he was talking about. Annabel had hit a nerve. 'Everyone's heard those stories. They're a tragedy. Kids are being taken advantage of, being taken from their homes. As you asked, yes it is something that Share the Love is spending money trying to solve, but it's an uphill struggle. Money is one thing, but what we need is collaboration with the government. At the moment, the government can't even collaborate with itself. There's so much corruption. That's why I wanted the money with Mum and Dad. I don't want it falling into the wrong hands.'

At that moment a door off to the side of the vast space opened and a man in his late fifties walked in.

'Ms Green, good to see you again.' It was Ousman, Emmanuel's manager. 'Manny, I hope you've been saying good things, eh?'

Annabel looked to Emmanuel, who was staring resolutely at the floor.

'Of course, Ousman — what else is there to tell?' His voice had gone low, quiet as Ousman came into the room. Annabel had never met the man before, Emmanuel's publicist had organised her previous meeting with him. She took an instant dislike to him, in part because of how clearly he seemed to be affecting Emmanuel, but also because he carried an air of aggression. The way he had bowled into the room and interrupted their conversation was an obvious attempt to put a halt to proceedings.

'Annabel, I'm sorry to do this but I really must insist that you go now. Emmanuel has a big training session tomorrow and needs to keep his energy up. I can see that you're already trying to get him drunk,' Ousman looked towards the empty bottles of beer on the table, 'What's your game? Trying to get him to say things he'll regret in the morning?' There was malice in his words. 'Emmanuel, it's time to see Ms. Green out. You need your beauty sleep.' Ousman stood over them and placed a firm hand on Emmanuel's shoulder, causing the man to wince. Emmanuel was not a small man, in fact he was built more like a rugby lock-forward than a footballer. He outsized Ousman by a great deal, but he was clearly physically threatened by him.

'Bit early for bed isn't?' Annabel checked her watch. It was still mid-afternoon.

'Sure thing, Ousman, we were just wrapping up anyway,' Emmanuel raised his face to meet Annabel and she couldn't discern what she saw there. Fear, yes, but there was something in his eyes, as though he were pleading her for help. Could it be that Emmanuel, shipped over to Europe to play football on a dodgy visa, risen to the top of the international circuit, was still under the influence of the gangsters who'd brought him here? Despite all his money and influence, could he still be being bullied by these men? Surely the only way for that to be the case must mean some threat to his family back in Senegal, Annabel thought. She was conscious of not overstaying her welcome, but also couldn't bear to be in the same room as Ousman for much longer. The guy was a slimeball, but something a lot more dangerous rippled just beneath the surface. He seemed capable of sudden, brutal violence, and that wasn't something Annabel wished to test.

'Of course,' she said, standing up and packing her things into her bag, 'I should be going, anyway. I left my taxi waiting outside. The fare's going to be astronomical.'

'Please,' Ousman said, 'Send me the bill. I'll cover the cost. Thanks for coming out all of this way.' Then, to Emmanuel, 'You stay sat, friend — I'll see Ms. Green out.'

Ousman moved away from behind Emmanuel and took Annabel by the elbow as he guided her forcefully towards the door.

'Thank you very much for your time, Ms. Green. I trust you have everything you need?' Ousman said as he opened the front door to the house. 'I think that should be enough time with my client for the foreseeable, yes?' The look in his eyes was cold, hard. There didn't seem a lot of point in arguing. But the fact that Ousman was closing off contact with Emmanuel sent up a red flag.

'Perhaps if I have anything else, I'll email?' She couldn't resist pushing back a little.

'Perhaps not,' Ousman said, struggling to maintain the polite smile that failed to reach his eyes. 'As I say, Ms. Green...

Annabel… I think you have everything you need.' Then, louder, so Emmanuel could hear, 'We look forward to seeing the piece hit the headlines, finally — don't we Manny?' Annabel looked back to see Emmanuel nod gently, his eyes closed.

With that, he placed his hand on the small of her back and forced her through the door, slamming it behind her.

Her head raged. She knew a veiled threat when she saw it. Every biological instinct told her she should flee, drop that line of enquiry immediately. But she had honed her journalistic instinct to override her body's propensity for self-preservation. She had rattled Ousman, which meant she was onto something.

14

Daylight broke through the flimsy fabric Afam had used to make a curtain for the attic window. The light did its best to pierce his eyelids. He rolled over on the futon mattress he'd placed on the floor, pulling the sheet tight around him. It was futile, he was awake now. He looked over to the travel alarm clock he'd placed on top of a pile of old magazines he had found. Five thirty. Despite having gotten a decent night's sleep, it always felt as though he'd been up all night if he woke up before six.

Afam reached for the glass of water next to the alarm clock and pulled the switch on the ornate table lamp he'd perched on his makeshift bedside table. The lamp cast an oppressive glow over everything, the wattage of the bulb barely strong enough to make it through the thick brocade shade. He hauled himself up to a seated position and rubbed at the back of his neck, working out the knots that had formed overnight. He shuffled down to the end of the mattress and pulled on his socks and sneakers. As he moved his way over to the attic hatch, he grabbed his hoodie from the back of a chair, failing to stifle a cough as he disturbed one of the white sheets that had been draped over the collection of antique furniture like ghosts.

Fully dressed, he hoisted up the hatch in the floor that served as his bedroom door and descended the ladder onto the first floor landing. He made his way down the stairs into the kitchen, being careful to avoid the floorboards that creaked, though it always seemed that new ones popped up overnight to trick him as he went about his morning ritual. After a glass of water and a banana to break his fast, he grabbed his keys from the hook beside the door, stuffed them into the pocket of his training pants and made his way out onto the street.

There was a chill in the air outside and Afam flicked the hood of his sweatshirt up, pulling the drawstring tight. He found he was actually quite fond of the weather in Paris, despite how different it was to back home. In the time he'd been here, though, he still hadn't quite become used to the morning chill. He retrieved his phone and fired off a quick message to Iman, then pulled out his headphones and plugged them into the headphone jack of the device. His running playlist was a mix of music from home and some tracks that his housemates and colleagues had introduced him to and he felt his heart rate increase as the beats and the bass filled his ears. As he shook the cobwebs out of his bones, Afam noticed movement from the corner of his eye. It had been a few weeks since the ordeal of his border crossing, since the men who were supposed to help him had assaulted him. He had expected that they would have been keeping tabs on him, but so far he'd seemed to have evaded them. But still his nerves were on edge at every inexplicable noise, every person who loitered too long outside his house. Paris was a big city, and he'd ended up out in the suburbs. Still, part of him knew it was only a matter of time.

Afam turned and moved towards the side of the house where the disturbance had come from. As he made his way to the row of trash cans in the alley beside the house, there was another flash of movement and someone was moving towards him out of the darkness. Afam's body tensed, his pulse quickened. All of his senses were on high-alert, his subconscious mind making split-second decisions on whether to stay and fight, or to flee. His hands balled into fists and he strode forwards, towards the threat.

'*Bawo ni*, brother,' the stranger said, and the Yoruba phrase threw Afam. He had been hard at work learning the French language and had worked on not falling back on English as much as was possible, so it felt strange to hear words from home when he was still so far from there. Afam squinted into the darkness.

'Leye?' Afam felt his legs begin to wobble and took a seat on one of the nearby bins, 'Is that you?'

'Afam! You would not believe how long I've been looking for you.' Leye was leaner and wore the burdens of his exile heavily. His hair had not been cut for several weeks and there was more than a five o'clock shadow across his face. His weight loss emphasised the bags under his eyes, which seemed to have sunk deep into his skull.

'What the... how did you even...' Afam was lost for words. He hadn't known where he was going to end up — how had Leye come to find him in the suburbs of a cosmopolitan capital city halfway across the world. 'I though you went to live with your cousin?' Afam suddenly remembered why they'd both had to leave home.

'I did, but... well... it didn't quite work out.'

'What do you mean?' Afam asked.

'All in good time, brother, but let's just say his boss didn't really appreciate my advances on his daughter.'

Afam couldn't help but laugh. He shook his head.

'Hey, man, it takes two to tango,' Leye continued, 'She wasn't so innocent herself. A strong independent woman. Old enough to make her own choices.'

'Please tell me you didn't say that to him?' Afam teased.

'You're kidding me, right? I wouldn't be here if I'd have done. Or, well, I might have been here, but my balls definitely wouldn't be!' Leye burst into laughter at his joke.

Afam had joined in with his old friend, but time was ticking, 'You're going to make me late for work.'

'Typical Afam,' Leye said, rolling his eyes, 'Comes all the way to Paris and ends up clearing up other people's shit for no pay.'

Afam's brow crinkled. There was a new bitterness in his old friend.

'What else could I do?' Afam said, and turned on his heels, 'Come on, I mean it. I don't have time to just stand here in the middle of the street. We can talk on the way in.'

Afam pocketed his headphones and set off down the road at a light jog, leaving Leye staring at his back as he moved off into the distance. Leye rolled his eyes, cracking a small smile and set off after Afam as the rising sun began casting an amber glow across the surrounding buildings.

* * *

'So what are you doing here? How in God's name did you find me?'

Leye had just about managed to keep pace with Afam, and the two had pounded the pavement in silence as the rest of the world woke up around them, the only sound the slap of their shoes on the asphalt and Leye's laboured breath. Afam wiped a sheen of light, dewy perspiration from his brow and laughed inwardly as he watched Leye doubled over, sucking in huge gulps of breath.

'It's a long story,' Leye said, 'But as I say, things didn't work out at my cousin's. I kept my head down there for a while, and started working for some friends of his,' he held out a placating hand to Afam, 'Nothing illegal, don't worry. Well, not too illegal. No drugs or guns or anything, just running errands for the guys.'

Leye paused, anticipating a comment from Afam but none came.

'But then I got talking to his daughter. She was very beautiful. One thing led to another, you know... it was okay for a while, but then he caught us. Chased me out of town in my underwear. I'm lucky he didn't kill me... so anyway, after that I went back home... Relax!' Leye responded to his friend's shocked expression, 'Not 'home', home. I stayed out of the way, didn't go anywhere near AJ. But then one day I ran into Blessing, you know the girl in Iman's class. She told me you'd sent Iman an iPad, paid for by your new job in Paris at some football club. So I spoke to Moses and... well, you know what happened after that. When I finally made it here, I figured you'd never have made it to PSG, so I just went looking. I walked miles around this place, slept outside a few nights. I followed you home last night.'

'You should have let me know, Leye. You didn't need to sleep on the street,' Afam said, shaking his head in disbelief. 'You could have found a way to let Iman know. She could have told you where I was...'

'How about that crossing, eh?' Leye carried on, changing the subject, 'The water just seemed endless. I felt like I was seasick most of the way. I kissed the ground when we got to the other side.'

'Did everyone make it?' Afam asked. Like everyone else, he'd heard the horror stories of migrants crossing the sea in capsized boats.

'In my boat, yes. The water was very choppy. We tipped over, but it was just young guys on the boat,' Leye said, 'We weren't that far from the shore and paddled our way to safety. Lucky there were no kids or anything otherwise who knows what would have happened. The sea was terrible; so much of it every way you look, even down.' A shudder ran through Leye's body as he remembered the fear that had shot through him when he had looked down into the murky depths of the strait. The water was crystal clear around his hips, legs, feet, but soon after that the light refracted and the water took on a gloomy quality. He had no idea how deep down it went. What those depths held.

'So what happened to you?' Leye asked, and it felt to Afam like he didn't care about listening to the answer. Despite this, Afam launched into the full story of his travails. He told Leye about the long trip crammed into a crate in the back of a truck, the men with guns. When he started telling Leye about Awusi and the kids a smile spread across his face as he remembered playing games with Effia, keeping her busy on the long journey. And her brother, who had slept the whole time. A small blessing for Awusi as she navigated the awful choices in front of her. His heart sank when he remembered that he hadn't seen a reply to the email he had sent as soon as he'd got his phone. He hoped they had found somewhere safe. He wondered if he'd ever get to see them again.

'So, listen,' Leye spoke up as Afam had gone quiet, 'Can I stay with you? Looks like a nice house you've got there. Lots of room.' He raised his eyebrows in an affected gesture.

Afam paused for a long moment. He had landed on his feet here. Something about Leye coming back into his life had shaken him. Something about his story didn't quite sit right, about his work with the gangsters who had trafficked Afam into France. Iman had said that Area Boys had been loitering around their house, asking where he was, saying he still owed them money for setting him up abroad. Part of him feared that Leye had gotten too tangled with them. Would he sell Afam out? Even if Leye was telling the truth, Afam had tried very hard to put what had happened — in AJ City, during the crossing, his arrival in Paris — behind him. Seeing Leye had brought it all crashing back.

'You can stay for a few nights, of course, but I'll have to speak to the guys about anything longer than that.'

'The guys?' Leye asked.

'It's not just mine, dummy,' Afam said, laughing, 'I share the house with some of the guys from the club.'

'Ah! Here was I thinking you'd made it big,' Leye said, 'Of course, ask the others. You're a life saver. I'm not sure I could take many more nights roughing it out here — it's so cold in Europe! Make sure you tell them what a good guy I am. I could get a job to cover my costs. And then try to get a ticket back home.'

Afam's heart ached when he thought of home, but he had discussed it with his family — he was on a good track at the club. He was training with the youth team and was picking up cash-in-hand shifts on the maintenance team as well, which was the only way to get around the fact he couldn't get legitimate work without papers. The money paid for his bed and board and most of the rest he sent home. It was enough to cover Iman's school fees, which meant that she didn't have to drop out and work to put food on the table. It also left some for the rest of the family, meaning that his mom didn't need to work quite so hard either.

When he had first called Iman, he had tried to get some information on the crash but she hadn't known anything. He hadn't wanted to push in case she became suspicious. Even if he worked enough to afford a ticket home, he didn't have a passport. He would have to contact the authorities, would have to tell his story. Moussa had helped him apply for asylum, but what questions would the authorities ask if he wanted to go home again? Wouldn't it bring up questions about why he left in the first place? He still wasn't sure how effectively he could lie under that sort of pressure — massaging the truth for Moussa and the club was one thing, but immigration agents would smell a rat from a mile off.

'Afam,' Leye was waving his hand in Afam's face. Afam blinked rapidly, shook his head. 'Where did you go?'

'Sorry, sorry... what were you saying?'

'The key,' Leye said, 'Can I have your key so I can let myself in and have a shower?' He pulled at the collar of his t-shirt, performed an elaborate sniff and screwed up his face.

'Sure,' Afam laughed, and dug the key out of his pocket, 'Leave it behind the trash cans so I can get in later on. I've got training after work.'

'You mean my old bed?' Leye joked, 'Sure thing. It's good to see you again, Afam. I knew you'd be there for me.'

'Have a shower, get some sleep. See you later, Leye.'

Leye took the key from Afam and headed for the main door. As he crossed the parking lot, he heard the high pitched revving of a scooter engine and looked up. The driver of the scooter stared at Leye and raised an inquisitive eyebrow. Leye met his gaze and nodded. A vicious smile spread across the man's face and he pulled on his helmet, kicked the scooter into gear and sped out of the car park.

15

'We need to talk.'

Afam hadn't noticed Vincent sit down next to him. He was consumed in his music, laid back on the couch, headphones strapped to his ears. Vincent grabbed Afam's foot and shook it, making his housemate jump. Afam pulled down his headphones, the tinny metronome of a hip hop drum track crackling out into the air.

Vincent had just been promoted into the squad from the academy. He was about the same age as Afam, and had grown up in the local area. Afam didn't get much opportunity for down-time outside of work and training, but the few times that he and his housemates had gone out to the local bar, Vincent had been cock of the walk — everyone wanted to say hello to him. Later on in the evening, this had proven very effective as a group of attractive young women joined them at their table. Afam had spent the night flirting and buying drinks for one of them, Roxanne, and the two had stayed in touch afterwards. They had arranged a date for a few weeks later, in the city at one of Roxanne's favourite bistros.

'Hey, Vinny... what's up?' Afam said, still trying to get his bearings slightly.

'We need to talk,' his housemate repeated.

'Sure, what's up?' Afam asked again, apparently oblivious to Vincent's tone.

'It's Leye,' Vincent blurted this out as though he'd been working himself up to say it. He paused before he continued, not quite meeting Afam's eyes as he spoke, 'Well, at least I think it's Leye. It might be. I don't want to be a dick, Afam, but stuff keeps going missing. Some of Guillame's records have disappeared and Robert's sure that he's missing some clothes. Couture stuff...'

'Are you sure he's not just left it on the floor of some guy's room?' Afam laughed, but Vincent didn't return the smile.

'And now my watch. Scratch that, my grandfather's watch. It's gone. Sure, the other stuff's small, it might have got lost, but I never let that watch out of my sight, Afam — you know that.'

'So what?' Afam asked, trying not to sound too defensive, but finding it difficult to keep his temper under control, 'You've lost your stuff and now it's Leye's fault? I know he's a bit rough around the edges, Vincent, but he can't help that. You don't know the half of what we've been through, or where we come from. You think you grew up with nothing? You don't know how good you have it. So what if I ask Leye and we find out it wasn't him? Who's next for the accusation? Me? Because I'm as rough around the edges as he is, Vincent.'

Vincent sighed. 'I don't know, Afam. I like Leye, he's a fun guy, but what I do know is that he came here and stuff started going missing. Look, I don't want to fall out with you about it. Just talk to him, please? The others want his head. I said I'd talk to you. I know you want to settle this in a civil way.'

'Sure,' Afam said, still trying to compute what he was being told. He was surprised at how offended he felt, and how he had immediately jumped on the defensive. But it was true, Leye had always run with a shady crowd, but the boy he knew was honest to the bone, not a petty thief.

* * *

'Honey, I'm home,' Leye called out as he let himself through the hatch to Afam's attic bedroom. With some rearranging, they had fit another single mattress through the opening and this now served as Leye's place to crash. Afam's housemates had been wary at first but Leye had ingratiated himself with the group. He was also usually out for most of the day — Afam didn't know where — and tried not to encroach too heavily on the shared living spaces. He also contributed a little money towards rent and utilities. Whilst he'd kept his presence light in the house downstairs, the attic was a different story. Empty wrappers and food cartons littered the unmade bed. It looked a lot worse in juxtaposition to Afam's side of the room; everything with a place and in its place.

Afam put down the newspaper he had been reading and closed his eyes, massaging them with his thumb and forefinger. He had been reading a story about Emmanuel Diouf, who had been involved in an accident at home that had resulted in him breaking his leg and several ribs. A picture of Diouf accompanied the article, and his face was a bruised and battered mess. He was going to be out of the game for months, which at his age essentially signalled the end of his career. Footballers didn't get much time in the sun, Afam pondered, which is why it was so important for him to give this opportunity everything he had.

Afam squeezed his temples and drew his fingers together across his brow, where he held the bridge of his nose. He had been preparing for this conversation for a few days but hadn't managed to get a moment alone with Leye since he'd spoken to Vincent. Now he had found Leye, he couldn't bring himself to speak. Couldn't bring himself to ask his oldest friend if he had been stealing from their housemates.

'Okay...' Leye extended the last syllable, confused by his friend's silence. He sense that Afam was gearing up to say something,

something apparently serious, yet was unable to take Afam's solemn expression seriously.

'Where's the watch?' Afam said, biting the bullet.

'What do you mean? You want to know the time?'

'Don't bullshit me, Leye. I know what the time is. It's time for you to be honest. These people you're stealing from, they're my friends. You have been welcomed into this house and have thrown charity back into these people's faces.'

'Whoa, whoa,' Leye interjected, 'Slow down. Who's stealing what now?'

'Vincent's watch. That his grandfather gave to him. It's missing.'

'And I'm supposed to have taken it?' Leye feigned offence, spreading an open palm across his chest.

'Well, the timing is right... It's not just the watch either. Other little things. It's too much for it to just be coincidence, Leye. Be honest with me, I'm your friend.'

'Is that right?' The conversation was taking a bad turn from the outset, 'A friend who takes the side of others? I'm not sure you and I have the same idea on what friends are, brother.' Leye's face had curled up into a snarl, his upper lip creased up towards his nose. 'Let me tell you what friends do, Afam. Friends look out for each other. They keep one another safe. Friends keep secrets for one another.' He let his last point hang in the air between them. Afam's heartbeat raced, adrenaline coursed through him. He breathed deeply, counteracting the emotions rising in his heart. His hands clenched into fists.

'What are you talking about, Leye? You know I've kept that secret as well as you have. We both have as much to lose in letting the truth come out.'

'We do?' Leye said, 'Is that true, Afam? Look around you. It's not much, but this is yours. All I've got is a filthy mattress in the corner like a dog. And what have I got at home? Less. Don't pretend for a second that I've got as much to lose as you have, brother. You have your life, opportunity... family.'

'What do you mean, family?' Afam was having trouble containing his rage now. Leye's apparent discontent had taken him by surprise. 'Is that a threat? You are a brother to me, to Iman. A son to my mother. We've fed you, given you a bed.'

'Relax, Afam,' Leye grinned, 'You're getting a little hot under the collar. It's no threat. But think what it would do to your sister if you got found out. She'd be screwed. She'd be ashamed of you, sure. But without big bro watching her back, sending her to school, she'd soon have to find another way. Find a nice husband. She's a pretty girl, I'm sure she wouldn't have much trouble.'

'Who the fuck are you, man? That's my sister,' Afam was yelling now, 'She may as well be your sister. I don't know what happened to you whilst you were with your cousin and his friends, but I don't like it.' He was on his feet now, pulling a sweatshirt over his head, stuffing his keys into his pockets. 'You've changed. You're so full of hate...' A glint of confusion furrowed Afam's brow as he searched for his next words. 'Look,' he spoke slowly, catching his breath, bringing himself under control word by word, 'I don't care what you stole, just get it back. Or get the fuck out.'

Afam pulled his hood over his head and walked to the hatch in the floor, descending the fold-out staircase like a well-practised submariner and headed down the staircase, through the front door and out onto the street.

Leye waited until he heard the door slam before reaching for his phone — a battered old Nokia handset — and tapping away at the keys. The whoosh of a text message being sent sounded, and he pocketed the device again. It only took a few seconds before the phone vibrated in his pocket, followed by the soprano morse code that indicated a reply. He didn't bother to check what it said, he already knew. They would be watching him. They always were.

Afam pounded the pavement. He had set off from the house at a brisk walk, trying to shake off the remnants of his fight with Leye.

He couldn't believe this version of the man he'd known since they were both too young to remember. Exile had changed him, had turned him hard, cold. Made him forget where he'd come from, the promises they'd made one another not to fall in with the wrong crowd. In only a few weeks Leye had gone from beloved brother to petty thief, stealing from the people who'd given him shelter in his time of need.

Afam had forgotten to grab his headphones, so he listened to the sounds of St Ouen as he ran. There was little but traffic noise. Barely anyone on the streets. Most of the residents had worked themselves to the bone all day, the idea of spending all evening in the local bars and cafes was a long way off. There were, of course, a few of the same old barflies wafting around Phillipe's bar near the stadium, filling up the ashtrays set on the plastic garden furniture, shooting the breeze about the weather, politics, football. Afam shot a quick wave at Phillipe as he ran past, and the barman yelled something good-natured but indistinguishable as he sped past.

Afam had picked up the pace, was driving his feet into the tarmac, propelling himself forward. The thud of his soles reverberated off of the buildings all around and he began to lose all sense of his surroundings. His legs felt as light as air, as though they could carry him like this for days. He pumped his arms in rhythm with his legs, his jagged breaths matching the movement of his body. He never noticed the outstretched leg. It took him a few moments to realise he was falling. His arms had come up instinctively, breaking his fall as he thudded to the ground. He heard laughter, spun his head towards it, but it felt like everything around him was taking a few seconds to catch up.

He pulled himself up to sitting, the palms of his hands throbbing where he'd caught his fall. A warm trickle of sweat ran down his forehead, but when he raised his hand to touch it, it came back red.

He reached his hand up to the source of the bleeding and winced at the pain.

'Sorry, man, didn't see you there,' a voice emerged from the confusion. Laughter from several people.

Afam started to stand but a vicious blow struck him in the rib cage, knocking the wind out of him and sending him sprawling to the pavement once more. He cried out in pain, covered his head with his hands instinctively. More laughter now, like a pack of hyenas.

'Stay down,' the voice piped up again, barking the order. Afam felt movement on his right, felt the pressure change in the air as another body drew close. 'Did you think we wouldn't find you?' The voice was closer now as the man crouched down to Afam. He recognised the man speaking, racked his brain desperately seeking an explanation to what was going on.

'You see, Afam, we've been searching. And then when we found you, we watched you. Watched your family. Iman, she's clever no? And pretty. She'd make someone a good wife one day, I think.' The man said, echoing words Afam had heard Leye say moments before.

'You stay away from her!' Afam found his voice and launched himself up onto his feet, stumbling a little as the blood rushed to his head. Hands grabbed his arms on either side. He pulled hard against the grip but they held strong. He brought his eyes up to meet his attacker.

'You've got a lot of fight, Afam. I like that,' Isaac said, 'Could put that to good use. What do you say?'

'What do you want? You already took everything.'

'Everything? Come on now, Afam. We've been watching you for a while now. Quite the entrepreneur, eh? Made a good thing out of a bad situation. Of course, you're cleaning up other people's shit, but we all have bills to pay...' Isaac paused, raised a finger in the air as though something had just struck him, 'Which reminds me, bills to pay... you realise how much it cost to get you here, don't you? Extraordinary amounts of not just cash, but time and personal effort — hard to put a price on that, isn't it?'

'I already paid you, before I came here. I paid Moses,' Afam said, finally realising what was happening.

'Do I look like Moses? Don't answer that. You paid some of what you owe,' Isaac rubbed his index finger and thumb together, 'But now you're earning, Afam, we've come to take the rest.'

'There's nothing to give. It's a little cleaning job. I barely make--'

'Tut tut,' Isaac shook his head, 'Now a little bird tells me your sister has a brand new iPad she's flashing around at school. You know better than I do that's not the sort of thing collecting bottles affords you.'

Afam had to play this carefully. Clearly they had someone watching his family in Lagos. A wrong move here would almost definitely mean repercussions for them. 'What do you want?' he conceded.

'Very wise, Afam,' Isaac said, 'Commission. Twenty points on everything you make.'

'Twenty?'

'I know, it's not much but we are not greedy men, Afam. Who knows, on top of this we may need you to do some stuff for us one day... but we'll come to that when we come to that.'

'I can't work for you! If they ever found out I was involved in any of your business, I'd lose my job. I'd lose my chance in the squad. I'd lose my right to stay in the country,' Afam saw an opportunity to gain the upper hand, 'And then where would you be? If I can't stay here, I can't earn, and if I can't earn there's nothing for you to gain. Twenty percent of a shopping cart filled with plastic doesn't put much food on the table.'

At this huge peals of laughter erupted from the men.

'Madman. You think these people are still interested in you playing for them? They've got you on the hook, Afam — they don't need to give you anything. You're grateful for what you've got. Before long you'll be too old, you'll have missed your chance. Then what? You going to clean up after your 'friends' for the rest of your life?'

Afam opened his mouth to reply but the words wouldn't come. The seeds of doubt Isaac had sown immediately stuck in his throat.

'Here,' Isaac said, 'Ten points, Afam. I'll know if you short me. And keep this.' He held out an ancient, battered mobile phone in his outstretched hand.

The men released their grip on Afam's shoulders, allowing him to reach forward for the device. 'Don't call us, we'll call you, yeah? Tell Leye we said "hi" as well.'

Afam stumbled forward as the two men who had been holding him barged through him to join Isaac, who turned away from Afam. The three men raised their hoods, pulled the brims of caps down low to obscure their eyes and made their way over to a car Afam recognised as the one that had picked him up from the train station.

What did Isaac mean about Leye? They must have been watching the house if they knew he was here as well. Afam's mind raced at the various implications. He pocketed the mobile Isaac had given him, turned on his heel and sprinted back home as fast as his heels would carry him.

16

As Afam crashed through his front door, his chest heaved with the exertion from the run home. His mind had not stopped racing as he'd sprinted the entire way home. If they were watching the house that put them all at risk. He would have to tell Vincent and the guys. They already knew where he worked. But worse than all of that, they knew about Iman, knew about the iPad he'd sent back home so he could call and see them whenever he liked. Iman hadn't said anything. She was wise enough to spot that sort of danger, she would have mentioned something. At least he hoped she would. Hoped she wasn't so scared by something that she didn't feel she could tell him about it.

Laughter erupted from the front room. Leye's unmistakable cackle, but accompanied by Vincent's dulcet rumble. Afam took deep lungfuls of air, each breath calming him, bringing his heart rate down. He tossed his keys onto the bureau in the hallway and checked his reflection in the mirror. Dry blood caked the right side of his face and he spat on the corner of his sleeve and rubbed at it, turning the fabric a dull grey-pink. He pulled the jumper off, wiped the sweat off of his face and moved through to the communal room.

The shared living space was fairly chic, kitted out with reproduction vintage and antique furniture. Tasteful vintage movie posters adorned the walls alongside a few signed replica football shirts. A huge wide-screen TV hung on one wall above a media station that contained an expensive SONOS wireless speaker and several computer games consoles. A large, low coffee table sat between the television and the L-shaped mock-velour sofa that took up the majority of the floor-space in the room. The table stood as a reality check for the otherwise tastefully 'footballer chic' decorated house. The palette was all shades of grey and beige. Empty bottles of beer and crumpled cigarette packets were slung across the tabletop, shoes and socks discarded at random around the seating area. The dining table towards the kitchen area was more of a dumping ground for training kits, with half-dried athletic wear draped over the backs of chairs or bundled on top of sports holdalls.

The kitchen, intended to be a monochrome and stainless steel culinary temple, was instead an extension of the coffee table, with more beer bottles and half-eaten meals taking up the majority of the space on the worktops. The rumble of the dishwasher at least suggested that someone was attempting to make headway on the cleaning.

'Hey, Afam...' Vincent looked up as he came in, performing a brief double-take at his housemate's ragged appearance, '... everything okay?'

Afam plastered on a smile. Vincent was laid out on the couch, games controller in hand, the game paused on the big screen. A half empty glass of wine sat on the coffee table in front of him, a magazine tossed down beside him, open on a glossy advert depicting a well-dressed man on a yacht somewhere that looked like the Mediterranean. That same stretch of water looked so different to the one he had experienced.

'All good, all good...' Afam trailed off.

'What's with the... ' Vincent continued, raising a questioning finger to his eyebrow.

'Oh,' Afam had hoped his quick cleanup job would detract attention from the wound, stop him having to answer awkward questions. Telling more lies. 'I fell.' A half truth. 'Running too hard, I guess.' From what? he asked himself.

'This guy never knows when to call it quits,' Leye joined in now, 'That's how I've always known he's going to be a star.' He stood up and moved over to Afam, planting a palm across his shoulders.

'You're not wrong, Leye — I've seen him on the pitch. Guy's unstoppable when he wants to be.'

Afam couldn't quite understand the change in attitudes until he spied Vincent's wrist, saw the delicate leather strap holding an elegant, understated gold watch face in place. His grandfather's watch.

Vincent noticed Afam staring.

'Ah, yeah. Look, sorry about before. I shouldn't have been so... indelicate. Leye explained everything to me and... well, look — no harm, no foul. I've got the watch back, I've got a glass of wine. Let's all just put it behind us, eh?'

Afam blinked, dumbstruck.

'Sure,' he eventually managed to force the words out, 'Sure, sorry, yes.' Afam continued to stumble through the words, 'Sorry, Vincent, I just need to talk to Leye in private.' He grabbed Leye's arm and started pulling him back out to the hall.

'Cool, no problem — I should get an early night, anyway. You guys stay here, finish the bottle if you want.' Vincent picked up his magazine and glass of wine, downing the last of his drink and placing the glass on the kitchen counter. 'Night, guys,' he said as he departed.

Afam stared deep into Leye's eyes as the two waited in silence, listening for the sound of Vincent ascending the stairs, the lock of the bathroom door and the hiss of the shower starting.

'You fell?' Leye asked, nodding at the wound above Afam's eye.

'Tripped,' Afam said, unconsciously raising his hand to dab at the cut, 'Look, let's cut the shit. I tripped because someone tripped me.'

'What do you mean?' Leye said, recoiling in shock, 'Someone attacked you?'

'Three guys. The same assholes who picked me up from the station when I got here. Same ones who stole my stuff and left me stranded. Friends of Moses.'

'What?' Leye's voice spiked above the whisper they were both maintaining, 'What guys?'

'I told you about them already. Isaac. I don't know what the other two are called. I don't even know if his name's really Isaac.'

'What did you do?'

'What could I do? They knew stuff, Leye. Too much stuff. Where I worked, where I live. They knew about Iman, about my mum, my brothers. They knew about you...'

'About me? What about me?'

'Who knows? Just as they left they told me to say hi to you. Something's not right here, Leye. We need to be careful. Do you think they might know your cousin?'

Afam watched Leye's face as his eyes darted all around the room, avoiding meeting Afam's gaze.

'How do I know? He knows a lot of people. Of course it's possible he might know people here. Modern technology, Afam — crime travels. People's power these days extends way beyond physical territory.'

'Well we need to sort something out. They're trying to extort me - he wants twenty per cent of everything I make...'

'Is that it?'

Afam couldn't believe Leye's response.

'What do you mean "is that it?" Isn't that enough?'

'All I mean, Afam, is that for a measly twenty percent of your measly wage, you could be safe. We could be safe. Iman could be safe.'

'Yeah, sure,' Afam said, 'Until they come back and want thirty. What then?'

'Is that not a small price to pay for peace of mind?'

'Peace of mind? Are you out of your mind? Gangsters are trying to extort me, threatening me, us, my family, and you're talking about peace of mind? Are you on their side or m--'

'Don't be so ridiculous,' Leye fired back, interrupting Afam, 'You know I've got your back. I've had your back for longer than we can both remember and in more ways than most.'

'Sure, but that was before.' Afam's blood was up and he was at risk of saying something he might regret. But he had to say something. 'Where have you been all this time, huh? Where did you go with that watch? How did you get it back so soon? You couldn't afford to buy that back from a fence.'

Leye paused, leaning in conspiratorially, 'Who says that's strictly true, Afam?'

'What?'

'Who says I don't have any money? I don't have a job, sure, but there are more ways to make money than having a job.'

'What the fuck are you talking about?' Afam said, and then, 'You are working for them! Unbelievable. These men are criminals, Leye. They are leeches, preying on us. Literally us — you and me. They exploit people back home. They exploit me. They threaten our mothers, our sisters. And you're working for them.'

'Oh, calm down, Saint Afam. What else am I going to do? Surely I don't need to remind you the events that led us here. I owe these people. We *owe* them.' Leye whispered through gritted teeth, spittle flecking out of his mouth as he spoke.

'I owe nothing to anyone!' Afam's voice rose, but he checked himself, not wanting to cause any more disturbance to his housemates. He paused, his eyes moved down for a few moments before he spoke again.

'You need to go.'

'What?' Leye answered.

'You need to go, now. Go now, come back in the morning — your stuff will be waiting for you. I won't.'

'Afam, come on, man. Let's not be hast—'

'Get out!' Afam grabbed Leye by the scruff and marched him towards the door. Leye put up little resistance. 'I bring you into my home and you bring with you these scum who threaten me, who threaten my family. The same family that treat you like a son, a brother. You need to go, now. And don't come back. We're done.'

Afam opened the door and thrust Leye out into the street, slamming the door before he had a chance to say anything more.

As Afam turned back into the house he looked up to see Vincent standing on the landing at the top of the stairs, towel around his waist, toothbrush hanging out of his mouth. Vincent cocked his head to the side, his eyes quizzical, but turned swiftly away as Afam fixed him with a death stare and pounded his way up the staircase, across the landing and up into the room above, pulling up the ladder and closing the hatch behind him.

Afam made swift work of throwing Leye's stuff into a duffel bag he had brought home from work. He scooped up Leye's meagre belongings, picking up fistfuls of clothes and dumping them into the holdall. Next, he moved over to the mattress and threw off the bedclothes, determined not to leave a single thing behind. He wanted nothing left in the house that would give Leye a chance to return, to worm his way back in and start again with his deceit.

As Afam swept his hand beneath Leye's pillow he felt a hard lump inside the cotton pillowcase. He picked it up and turned it inside out, tearing out the pillow inside. The hard lump fell to the bottom of the slipcase in his hand, weighing it down. Afam reached inside and found his hand wrap around cold steel, the ergonomics feeling like they fit his hand like a glove. He pulled his hand out, still gripping the steel, his brain somehow refusing to acknowledge what he already knew.

The handle and the bottom half of the gun was rough, designed for superior grip when firing. The tip of his index finger rested on the trigger whilst his thumb floated between the safety and the magazine release catch. He had seen enough bad cop movies to recognise a Glock handgun, the unmistakable silhouette of the standard issue US police force weapon. He aimed the gun up, looking down the sights, unable to help himself from flicking his aim around the room, feeling the power of the machinery in his hands. Such a small thing, really, but one that could cause such chaos.

A noise from the hallway of someone coming home snapped him out of his daze and he shook his head to clear his thoughts. He wrapped the gun back up in the pillowcase, shoved it into his own bag and lay back on his bed wondering what to do next.

It took Afam a few attempts to get through to Iman. The video connected, and he saw his sister sat in her room, looking flustered, bouncing her baby brother on her knee.

'Hey Afam, twice in one day? You really do miss us,' she smiled mischievously as she greeted him.

'Hey sis. Yeah, sorry. What took you so long, anyway? Everything okay there?' Afam felt exposed, like he was trying too hard to seem calm. He feared Iman would pick up on his unease immediately.

'Everything's fine. Well, apart from this guy,' she raised Azi up to the camera as he wriggled and squirmed, 'He's been a pain in the butt all day. Mom says she thinks he might have some teeth coming through, which is gross. Have to feel a bit sorry for the guy, though, must feel rough.'

The infant carried on squirming, vaguely focusing on Afam on the screen. Clearly he recognised him, but he couldn't quite compute how his big brother could be in the room and yet not be at the same time.

'Oof, poor guy,' Afam said, followed by a long, awkward silence.

'So...' Iman said eventually, trying to get her brother to reengage.

'Sorry,' he said, but again left it at that, finding it hard to find the words he needed.

'What's wrong, Afam? You're asking me if I'm okay, but it feels like you've got something going on. Two calls in one day. I can read you like a book, and not a very good book,' Iman joked. 'Are you sure you're okay?' He knew he could rely on her to see right through him.

'It's Leye. We had a fight.'

'Oh, not another of your lover's tiffs? Do you remember when you fell out over that girl and you didn't speak to him for about two weeks?'

'This is a lot bigger than that, Iman. A lot bigger.'

Iman noticed the heaviness in her brother's soul and switched to a more understanding tone.

'Tell me what happened.'

'First, I need to ask you something,' Afam said, 'I need to know whether you've had any trouble. You or mom. I know you say everything is okay, but I... look, I don't want to worry you, but I've heard a few things since Leye got here that make me worry. No one's come by the house, have they?'

'Afam, what are you talking about?' Iman's brow furrowed, 'Now you mention it, Moses came up to me the other day asking about you. They hang around with some of the girls there. Major creepy vibes. They're like twenty something, and these are fourteen-year-old girls.'

Afam's heart sank, he suddenly felt hollow.

'What did he say to you, Iman? What did Moses say?'

'Oh, nothing much. Like I say, he was being a total creep. Telling me I'd make a good wife, that sort of stuff. I ignored it.'

'Did he touch you? Did he hurt you?'

'No, no, chill. Like I say, I ignored it. He tried to put his arm around me, but I wouldn't let him. Then one of the teachers came out into the yard and he vanished, quick as a flash.'

Afam's palms felt cold and clammy, his anxiety was rising. He knew Iman was telling him the truth, but he saw more in what she had brushed off as the unwanted advances. It felt like a threat. A message to Afam. Do what we want or next time we won't give up so easily.

'So, what was your fight about?'

'Huh?' Afam had lost focus on the conversation.

'With Leye. You said you'd had a big fight. Something serious.'

'He's working with them. With Moses. With this guy in Paris, Isaac. Iman, I need to tell you something and I need you to swear that you won't tell anyone else.'

'Sure. I mean, I can't really promise that — like, what if you murdered someone? I'm not supposed to tell anyone about that?'

Afam paused again. He couldn't do it. How could he find the words to tell his little sister about what had happened to Sam? It would break her heart. Forever change their relationship.

'I...,' his throat felt dry and his next words caught in his throat. He swallowed hard, coughed, tried again. 'I... I never wanted it to go that far. It was just supposed to scare him. I don't know what we were thinking, how we could have thought it would end up any other way than it did...' Afam trailed off, the bravery he had briefly mustered spent up.

'Wait, what?' Iman said, the look on her face a mixture of confusion and horror. 'What are you talking about? You'd never hurt a fly, Afam. You could never kill someone. Who?'

'Samuel.' He let the name hang in the air.

'Again, who?' The revelation hadn't had the impact Afam thought it would, either that or Iman was trying to diffuse the shock.

'You don't remember him? The guy who used to hang around at the pitches. Used to give me and Leye rides around town...' he trailed off.

'Oh! Creepy Jesus guy. Yeah, he died in a car crash, didn't he? One of the girls in class, her brother was in the car when it crashed. He had his seatbelt on, but apparently that guy did not. Big mess.' Afam couldn't comprehend how casual Iman was being about his confession. It felt as though she wasn't taking him seriously. 'So that's the guy you apparently murdered? The one who died in that crash.'

'We clipped his brakes.'

A pause. 'You did what?' Iman finally sounded shocked, the reality of what her brother was saying finally catching up with her. 'Who's we? Leye?' Afam nodded. 'So that's why he crashed? Jesus... Afam... why?'

Typical Iman, Afam thought, even after such earth-shattering news, she still wanted to understand. Afam explained everything. It felt good to finally talk about it. He hadn't even spoken to Leye about what had happened. The only acknowledgement of their involvement in Sam's death had come through threats from Leye. Afam explained to Iman how weird Leye had been in the week or so that led to when Sam attacked Afam. Leye's rage when he found out Afam had been assaulted too. And then the morning that they had sneaked onto Sam's property and Afam had stood lookout whilst Leye rummaged around under his car.

'So you didn't actually do anything, then?' Iman interrupted Afam, 'It was Leye who got under the car. Leye who clipped the brakes. You stood lookout...' she paused then, and Afam didn't feel the need to fill the gap, he let her sit with the information, could see her cogitating, 'I mean, what you did isn't great, but you're not on the hook for this, Afam. Especially after what he did to you. To Leye. Who knows who else...' she paused, 'Wow, I wonder if that's why the kid was in the car. I bet he was grooming him as well. Lucky escape in more ways than one...'

'But a man died, Iman.'

'A man? A predator. An active sexual predator who over the space of a week had tried to assault at least two children... I wouldn't wish death on anyone, you know that. But few people would cry at Sam's funeral if they knew about what he'd been doing.'

Afam was taken aback. There was such a strange paradox in his sister's warmth, care and understanding about what had happened to him, what had driven him and Leye to do what they did, and the cold logic of her judgement of Sam. And she had taken so little time to come to a conclusion. Afam felt lighter having shed the burden of his secret, but also having Iman's perspective on events. It made him recalibrate his guilt.

'Listen, I have to go,' Iman said, breaking the silence that had emerged, 'I've got to help mom with dinner, and my homework isn't going to do itself. I'll speak to you soon, Afam. Stay safe. I love you.'

'Wait, Iman,' Afam said, 'Thank you.' And then, 'There's one more thing.'

'There's more?' Iman said, shaking her head in disbelief, 'Okay, hit me.'

'I told you, me and Leye had a big fight. I kicked him out of the house. Anyway, I was grabbing all his stuff and shoving it in a bag when I found something under his pillow.'

'Gross. Do I even want to know?'

'I'm serious, Iman. It was a gun. He had a gun bundled up in his pillowcase. Not a BB gun. A real, live gun, filled with bullets. I don't know what Leye has got himself caught up in, Iman, but it's not good. I don't know what to do.'

'With him, or the gun?'

'Both! I know he's in some deep doo-doo,' Iman laughed at her brother's infantile word-choice, 'And I know I should be trying to help him out of it, but it's like he was brainwashed in those few weeks he spent with them.'

'Either that or they've got something on him. They're holding something over him that means he has to do exactly as they say.'

'Like what?'

'Think Afam. What could they possibly know about Leye that he wouldn't want anyone finding out?'

The penny dropped and Afam felt like a fool. He had felt so confused, so threatened by the change in Leye that he hadn't stopped to think what might be causing it. Hadn't stopped to consider that the change in his behaviour wasn't simply some sort of moral decline. That the two of them could be in a very similar situation.

'Shit,' he said, 'I need to find him don't I?'

'That would be a good start.'

'Okay, since you seem to know everything. What do I do about the gun?'

'What about that woman?' Iman said, after racking her brains for a few moments, 'The one you told me about. The journalist you spoke to? She gave you her number right? Call her. She might not know what to do, but she probably knows someone who does. And besides, what's the alternative? Throw it away? Seems dangerous. And I'm not going to be the person who advises a black illegal immigrant to walk into a European police station with a gun.'

'Annabel?' Afam considered this for a moment, 'I mean, it can't hurt, I suppose. She seemed interested. Like she wanted to help me when I spoke to her. Worth a shot.'

'Okay, great. Now, Afam, I love you but I really do have to go. Stay safe. Don't do anything stupid. You're no use to anyone dead.'

'Okay, sorry, go. Say hello to the boys from me. And mom. And promise me, Iman, please — keep an extra eye out for any of these dodgy guys. I think they want something from me, and I don't want them to use any of you guys to get it. Just until I can clear everything up, be extra careful?'

Iman smiled, rolled her eyes. 'Yes, sir...'

'Please. Promise.'

'Okay, okay. I promise. Now let me go. And you go. Get some rest, big bro, you look terrible.'

With that, Iman leaned towards the camera and disconnected the call.

17

After her meeting with Diouf, and the encounter with his manager Ousman, Annabel was more determined than ever to find a link between the various parties involved in the human trafficking scandal that seemed to be simmering under the whole of French football. Whilst he hadn't explicitly said anything, it was clear that Diouf was under extreme pressure from Ousman. The way he had clammed up as soon as Ousman entered the room had spoken volumes, not to mention Ousman's veiled threat as she left Diouf's mansion.

She was no stranger to threats, it came with the territory — people with something to hide generally didn't like you snooping around. But Ousman seemed like a very nasty character. When she got back to her hotel room, the first thing she did was call David.

'Belle, would it not be better if you just came home? I'd feel a lot more comfortable knowing that you weren't stuck in some dingy hotel in Paris with the weight of a corporate behemoth and the Nigerian mafia bearing down on you.' She was touched that he felt the urge to protect her.

'Oh, so manly!' she joked, 'It's fine, David — I don't need you to protect me. He can make threats all he likes, but I'm not going anywhere. Just in case, though,' she paused, 'the man's name is

Ousman Diop. There's loads about him online. He's not an agent or anything. Has never done anything productive for Emmanuel as far as I can see, but seems to be living the life of Riley off the back of his 'friend's' success. I'm telling you, David, he's as bent as a nine-bob note.'

'Alright, Bill Sykes,' David mocked Annabel's use of the archaic phrase, 'But even if that's true, would it not be safer to sort it out from here?'

'You know as well as I do that you can get a lot more out of a face-to-face than you ever could through email or on the phone — people have nowhere to hide when you're right in front of them. Anyway, I think the Diouf thing is completely dead, obviously, but I think there might be something to that kid Afam I was telling you about. I think he might be a key piece in the puzzle. He gave me the same line of BS that Diouf did — got his chance through an academy, paid his way here. Only difference was there was no Ousman figure, no one else involved. Would an academy, even a dodgy one, send a kid all this way on his tod?'

'No. I don't think so.'

'Exactly. I think this Afam kid came here illegally, but like Diouf, he's made the best of a bad thing. I don't know whether he's still under the cosh, but if Diouf is anything to go by, there's bound to be something going on.'

David sighed. 'Just be careful, please. I don't want to turn into one of those sob stories about a man who lost his hero fiancée... and keep your phone on.'

'Will do. Don't worry about me, I'll be fine. Love you.' And with that, she hung up before he tried to convince her to come home again.

Annabel spent a few hours trawling through the data that Chloé had given to her on the thumb drive. She was searching for any correspondence that mentioned Georges Pepin, Ousman, or the man who had approached her in the lobby of the hotel, Félix. He hadn't given her his surname, which suggested to Annabel that his approach hadn't been above board. She had seen him a few more times as she'd been going about her business in the city and couldn't decide whether his conspicuousness was deliberate, or the result of his lack of guile. If it was the latter, she had little to worry about, though the former was a little more concerning.

She was hitting a brick wall, one that no amount of caffeine could conquer, and thought that a change of scenery would do her good. After a quick shower and some fresh clothes, she grabbed her bag and left the hotel into the Parisian evening.

Despite being generally underwhelmed by the city, she found it hard not to love any city at night. When the sun had set and the streetlights cast their halo on the streets below, a different sort of place came to life. Gone was the hustle and bustle of the rat race that plagued the metropolis and out came the night life. Restaurants and bistros filled with noise and merrymaking, the low thud of cocktail bars and clubs punctured the still night air as the urbanites came out in droves to slough off the stresses of the daytime. The city at night meant freedom, the anonymity often mocked by out-of-towners allowing people to forge their own path, unencumbered by what the neighbours might think.

Annabel made her way to the bistro that Chloé had recommended earlier that week. There was nothing particularly special about it, but she had enjoyed the kitsch atmosphere. There was a row of tables on the street outside the venue, covered with red gingham tablecloths, candles shoved into wine bottles dripping their wax down the sides, building another layer on top of countless others. Annabel took a seat at one of the tables and caught eyes with the same waiter who had served her days before. He acknowledged her with a curt nod as he carried plates of food to a neighbouring table and then went back inside the restaurant. A few moments later he had returned with a small glass of pastis alongside a small carafe of water and a bowl of ice cubes with a set of small tongs balanced on the edge. As the waiter spun off to attend another guest, Annabel added a few cubes of ice to her high-ball glass and half-filled it with water. The caramel-coloured liquid turned a pale, cloudy yellow and the pungent anise aroma filled her head, awakening her senses. She took a small sip and felt herself relaxing, the stresses from the story briefly forgotten.

The waiter returned and took Annabel's order without writing any of it down, something which impressed and terrified Annabel in equal measure. In fairness, there were three entrees on the menu and ten covers in the restaurant, so on balance it wasn't the greatest feat of memory but she still marvelled at how he managed to keep it up all night, every day of the week.

Annabel's food arrived. She felt exhausted by her extended stay in Paris and so had opted for a vast, comforting plate of *boeuf Bourguignon* which came accompanied by a fresh, crusty baton of bread and a half-carafe of house red. Annabel took a first bite, the tender, slow-cooked rump of beef falling apart in her mouth, the strong meat flavour mingling with the rich, earthy red-wine sauce and smoked speck, everything coming together to nourish her bones and protect against the chill in the evening air.

After a few more mouthfuls, Annabel got up from her table and, asking the waiter to keep an eye on her things, made her way to the bathroom. Emerging a short while later from what seemed to essentially be a janitor's closet with a toilet installed in it, she returned to her table which she found occupied by Félix. Noticing her at the door to the bistro, he looked up and delivered the same Cheshire-cat grimace she had seen in the lobby of her hotel.

'Ms. Green,' he said, spooning a portion of Annabel's food into his mouth. 'Sit,' he said, through a mouthful of food, indicating to the other chair at the table. He had abandoned all pretence of the charm he had flashed at their previous encounter.

Annabel took the seat opposite him and he continued. 'Ms. Green, my employer has it in his head that you are a dangerous woman. These past few days I have made it my business to ascertain quite how dangerous you are.'

'I'm flattered,' Annabel said, 'I've been called many things in my life, but I think 'dangerous' is a new one to me.'

'Cute,' Félix replied, a brief laugh escaping through his nostrils. He lit the cigarette between his lips, the flame of the match illuminating parts of his face but throwing others into deep shadow. 'But let's cut to the chase. It's getting late, it's getting cold. As much as you may come to know me as a cold, hard man, I am not immune to the pressures of the working week. I want to go home to my nice warm bed as much as the next man.' He took a sip of wine from Annabel's glass. 'You are to stop looking at Mr. Pepin. We have been lenient with you, so far, in part because my superiors are soft and believe in the integrity of a free press. They wanted to let you get bored and shuffle off on your own accord. Or scared. But you are getting too close to the fire. Free press or not, my employers do not wish for their private affairs to be made public. And they are not afraid to watch someone burn in order to keep their secrets. So let me tell you how things are going to work. You are to stop, with immediate effect. You are to destroy any and all evidence handed to you by Ms. Martin and any copies. You are to return to London where you will write your 'feel-good' piece about the immigrant footballer, or whatever it is you're supposed to be doing.'

'So I'm on the right track?' Annabel said, defiantly.

'Please, Ms. Green,' Felix took a long drag on his cigarette and blew the smoke out through pursed lips, like an overburdened parent trying to maintain their patience with an errant toddler. 'If you do not stop, then we will be forced to take alternative measures. You will not like these measures. They will make you wish that the worst thing that happened was you lost all of your journalistic credibility. Do we understand one another? We do not wish to escalate this situation. Do not force our hand. Do not end up like Ms. Martin.'

This jolted Annabel. 'What do you mean? What did you do to Chloé?' The threat suddenly felt very real.

'Relax,' Felix said, flicking ash from the tip of his cigarette into the ashtray on the table between them, 'Ms. Martin is fine. Well, physically at least. For now. But there is more than one way to skin a cat. Such a macabre English saying, don't you think? Ms. Martin already found herself knocked down a few pegs at work. She is at present undergoing a psychological evaluation to deem whether it will be necessary for her to attend some sort of rehabilitation facility. To the public, therefore, your story is based on little more than the ramblings of a mad woman with some sort of vendetta.'

'You can't do that, Chloé is an innocent woman. She's doing a public service in helping me get to the bottom of this story. People need to know what is going on. They will. And they will care.'

'But by that time, Ms. Green, Ms. Martin's word will be worth little more than any other mentally disturbed person. Destroying a person does not always necessitate a gross act of violence. At least not at first.'

'So is that what you're going to do to me,' Annabel asked. She was amazed at her ability to maintain a calm exterior when inside everything was racing a mile a minute, 'Destroy me?'

'In a word,' Felix took a final drag of his cigarette and directed a plume of smoke into Annabel's face. He stubbed the butt into what remained of Annabel's supper. 'Yes.' Félix stood up and grabbed his coat from the back of the chair he had been sitting in. 'Goodbye, Ms. Green. Think carefully about what we have discussed. If you are careful, then we can consider this adieu rather than au revoir... goodbye, Ms. Green. 'Til we meet again.' He turned on his heel and began to walk down the street. With sufficient distance between them, Annabel let out a breath she wasn't aware she'd been holding, her fingers uncurled from the can of mace she had stowed in the pocket of her jacket. Her eyes didn't leave Félix's back as he walked away into the distance, the clip of his leather soles resonating off of the surrounding buildings. Annabel's breath caught as he stopped dead in his tracks. He looked as though he were about to turn back to her, but then Annabel saw the flare of a match and a miasma of noxious cigarette smoke rose up around his head and he resumed walking. Annabel placed some Euros on the table, grabbed her bag and headed in the opposite direction.

18

Afam had sent a message to Annabel immediately after his call with Iman the previous evening and she had responded by the morning. They had arranged to meet at a cafe on the other side of town to St Ouen. Since his encounter with Isaac and his cronies, Afam was hyper-aware of his every move being watched so he wanted to put as much distance between his home and his meeting with Annabel as he could.

Afam didn't know if the gang knew about his connection with Annabel, but he wanted to protect her as it felt like she was the only person who could help him. He couldn't go to the police, as he was in the country illegally, and he had lied to Moussa about how he had entered the country — if Afam told the truth now he could be risking everything: his job, his chance at a career in football, and the freedom those things would deliver to his family.

Afam hadn't seen Leye since their last argument, but he was certain that Isaac would have ensnared him in his web once more, and that his old friend would be doing his bidding.

Afam had not slept well and so his run into work that morning was more of a light jog, his heart rate barely lifting above its resting state. The weather was beginning to turn, the chill in the air turning his breath to vapour in front of him, but also giving his mind a much needed sharpness, honing the fuzzy edges caused by sleep deprivation. He usually tried to avoid caffeine, but the thought of the coffee machine at work was spurring him on.

Afam wasn't the only one running this morning. One woman sped past him, hydration backpack strapped to her back, compression socks pulled high, her hair in a tight bun on top of her head. He tried to match pace, but he was no match for her lithe frame and soon she had an insurmountable lead on him, pulling ahead, seeming to match her pace with the ebb and flow of traffic so she didn't have to stop at any intersections. As he watched her fly off into the distance, Afam heard a voice to his right. At first he didn't register it properly, discounting it as just another element of the morning clamour — a labourer on a building site calling down to a colleague — but then he heard the voice again, more insistent this time. He felt his pocket buzz. The phone Isaac had given him.

He kept facing forward, desperate not to acknowledge the confrontation, hoping naively that ignoring the problem would make it go away.

'Afam,' Isaac called out, extending the second syllable of his name out in a mocking tone. Afam stared resolutely forwards, using his earbuds as cover.

'Afam,' he called out again, and Afam could hear anger seeping into his voice. The car they were in, the same slick BMW as before, was crawling the curb next to him, 'Come on now, don't be like that. What would Iman think of her sulking big brother...?'

This broke Afam's resolve, and he whipped his head towards the car. Isaac was leaning out of the passenger-side window, a malicious grin on his face.

'Got you,' he said, pointing his forefinger and thumb at Afam like a gun and cocking the thumb like the hammer of a pistol. Afam stopped running as the car pulled into the side of the road next to him. 'Get in.' The door opened and Afam saw the skinny man who had accosted him on his first day in Paris. He tapped the empty seat next to him. Afam looked up and down the street, but could see no viable escape route. He ducked his head, threw his bag into the footwell, and took a seat in the rear of the car.

* * *

They had driven around for around half an hour. Afam had tried to shrink as much as possible into his seat, fixing his gaze through the blacked-out windows. The music inside the car was deafening, and Isaac and his clique had to shout to be heard above the noise. For most of the journey they had chatted about nothing much — parties they'd been too, girls they had slept with, typical masculine bravado — but as they reached their destination, they turned their attention to Afam.

'So, Boy Wonder, this is how it's going to go down. We're going to get to where we're going soon, and when we do me and the boys are going to pop inside for a minute. Your job is to stand outside and keep watch. Leye told us you'd be the right man for the job. Got quite the track record there. Should be all good, but in case anyone starts poking their nose in that's what you're there for. Make them go away. And if anyone more serious shows up — like the cops — you let us know. We don't need anyone stepping on our business.'

'What do you mean, 'make them go away'?' Afam asked, not sure he wanted to know the answer and still reeling from Isaac's jibe about keeping watch. Leye had insisted he'd kept their secret.

'Here,' Isaac said, the unmistakable clack of a handgun slide being drawn back. He held out the weapon to Afam, who refused to take it. 'Don't be a pussy, Afam, I need to know you've got us.' He thrust the gun into Afam's hands and Afam stared at it, letting out a resigned sigh.

'Good boy. Now, let's go. Ready boys?' There was a murmur of assent from the occupants of the car and the doors began to open.

'Right, let's do this properly. Teach this connard to pay up on time.' They moved as one towards the front of the mobile-phone repair shop they had parked up outside.

'Afam, wait here, eyes on a swivel. Things might get a bit noisy.' Isaac pulled a balaclava down over his face and went inside the shop, locking the door from the inside as he went. It was only a few seconds before Afam heard the sound of smashing glass. He looked through the shop front and saw Isaac and his henchmen wielding sledgehammers and crowbars, smashing them down through the glass cabinets that displayed the mobile phones and electronic equipment that the shop had on offer. A middle-aged Indian man stood with his back against the wall, wincing with each blow. Isaac was pointing at the man, giving him a dressing down, as the others continued their wanton destruction. The shop owner nodded desperately as Isaac berated him, holding his gun up to the man's head. Afam felt sick at watching the violence. He felt hopeless, hated seeing the injustice but felt powerless to stop it. He turned away from the action inside the shop to survey the street. There were no pedestrians, and the few cars that drove past didn't seem to slow down at all as they passed.

Afam tried to gauge the distance to the corner, wondered if he could make it before the guys inside realised he was gone. But what was the point? They knew where he lived, where he worked, where his family was back home. It rooted him to the spot. The best he could do was make sure Isaac got out of the situation safely. Ensure he kept him in his good books. Perhaps then he would be lenient with Afam, let him keep his head down, pay his dues. The deafening report of a gunshot broke Afam's train of thought, followed by the incongruous tinkling of the shop bell as Isaac came tearing out of the shop.

He stopped in front of Afam, who stared in disbelief at the blood spattered on the front of Isaac's clothes. He cast his eyes inside the shop but could see no sign of the Indian man. 'I thought this was supposed to be a simple job?' he said to Isaac.

'Oops,' Isaac replied, with an exaggerated shrug, 'Come on, we're gone.' He shoved Afam, snapping him out of his shock, and the group all piled into the van. The engine roared to life, and the car moved slowly away from the curb, merging with the traffic.

'Shouldn't we get out of here?' Afam asked, panic rising in his chest.

'Chill, man,' said the driver, 'We are. No point speeding off, only makes people pay attention. Will be a long time before the feds get here, and we'll be long gone.'

As they made their way from the scene of the murder, Isaac turned around to face Afam.

'Phone,' he said, gesturing with his hand. Afam dug into his pocket and pulled out the burner that Isaac had given him, slapping it into Isaac's open palm. 'Merci.' Isaac said, and turned back into his seat, tapping out a number into the ancient handset. After a few moments the call connected.

'We need to switch cars. Bring the van. Meet us at the bridge.'

They drove for around twenty minutes, out onto the ring road that encircled the city. They were back out in the suburbs, but Afam didn't recognise anything. Eventually they came to a quiet area, and the car pulled across a dusty patch of scrub coming to a stop at the foundations of an off-ramp. They exited the car and made their way under the bridge where a battered, black VW Transporter was parked up. Afam stopped dead in his tracks when he clocked the man stood leaning against the bonnet.

'Afam. Long time no see,' Leye gave a curt nod, but then looked down at the ground.

Afam couldn't speak. He had spent a long time the previous night thinking about how to extricate the both of them from the situation with Isaac, and had come some way to accepting that Leye might not be an entirely willing participant in all that Isaac was making him do, but it still felt like a slap in the face to see him here.

'Come on,' Skinny shoved Afam from behind towards the back of the van. Afam climbed in and sat on one of the benches that was bolted to the chassis. He pulled his phone out of his bag and sent a brief message to Annabel. He was due to meet her in an hour but now he had no idea how long he would be stuck with Isaac. Leye entered the van and slid the door shut behind him. He took a seat on the bench next to Afam, as Isaac and the driver of the car entered the cab.

'Hey, what are you doing?' Skinny spoke up, his voice harsh and nasal. He had noticed Afam tapping out the message to Annabel, rescheduling their meeting.

'I was just texting my friend. I'm supposed to meet her soon, but it doesn't look like I'm going to make it, does it?' He couldn't help the bitterness in his voice.

'Are you dumb? You know what just happened right? No phones.' He snatched the phone out of Afam's hands, slid the door back open and tossed the handset out into the dirt.

'What's going on back there?' Isaac spoke up.

'Boy Wonder here was texting someone. Says it's some friend, but who knows?'

Isaac fixed Afam with an icy stare. 'Which friend?'

'Just some girl,' Afam said, which was only half a lie.

'Some girl? What girl? Leye,' Leye's ears pricked up, alert to an order from Isaac. Whereas before Afam had seen a new person in front of him, a criminal, living off of the misery of others, he now saw a desperation in Leye. He hung off of Isaac's words, desperate not to rub him up the wrong way, 'Who's this chick he's talking to?'

Afam watched Leye go over the possibilities in his mind. Any mention of Annabel the journalist would surely be cause for concern to Isaac and his boys.

'No one. Just some chick from work, right Afam? The one with the tits?' Afam breathed a sigh of relief. Leye's eyes connected with Afam's and the two shared a brief moment of recognition before the chirping of Isaac's mobile broke the tension in the air.

'Yeah,' Isaac started another monosyllabic conversation, 'Which one? Sure. Ten minutes.' He turned back to the load space where Afam, Leye and Skinny sat.

'New job, boys. Ousman wants us to pick someone up.'

'That prick, what are we, a taxi service for his whores?' Skinny spoke up.

'Not that kind of pick up, moron. Some woman refusing to wind her neck in. Wants us to shut her up. Come on, less talk, more action. Let's go.'

As the van moved off, Afam considered his ever-growing rap sheet. Not only was he an illegal immigrant, but in the space of twelve hours he had been implicated in a murder and was on his way to a kidnapping. He needed Annabel's help, now more than ever.

'Leye,' Afam heard Isaac's voice over the din in the back of the van, 'Bag him.' Before he knew what was happening a dark shroud fell over him. He struggled against the hood, but Leye held on tight. 'You want to be careful who you associate with, Afam. This lady journalist is a dangerous woman to know.'

'Just relax, Afam. Don't make it worse.' Betrayal. The last word that went through Afam's head before he felt a sharp blow to the side of his head and everything went dark.

***

Annabel sat at a corner table, her back to the bathroom, eyes fixed on the only entrance and exit to the bistro in which she'd arranged to meet Afam. It was a trick she'd learned from her dad, who'd told her about Wild Bill Hickok — he'd always sat in full view of the entrance to a room, in order that no one could sneak up on him. At a poker game, the only seat available was one with its back to the door. Forced to take the seat, with others at the table refusing to swap, Hickock was shot point blank in the back of the head. Annabel didn't think things would get as far as that, but better safe than sorry, she thought.

Her phone buzzed. It was Afam.

> Sorry. Been held up at work. Can we reschedule?

Annabel sighed and put her phone back in her bag before draining the last of her coffee. She had been hoping that the conversation with Afam would give her enough of a human story to bulk up the fairly tenuous claims about the international trafficking conspiracy. She hadn't been able to find any significant links between Georges Pepin and the fake academies, or between him and Ousman and the illegal gangs. All that work and the story was a non-starter. They had covered their tracks completely. Or maybe she had believed Chloe a little too readily and fallen down the rabbit hole.

She placed more than enough cash to cover the bill on their table and got up to leave. Her phone rang. She didn't recognise the number but answered anyway.

'Hello?' she said.

'Ms. Green,' Ousman's voice sent a shiver down her spine. 'Hope you're well. I wondered if you'd read the news?'

Annabel had slept late after being up all night trawling the documents from Chloe. She hadn't had time to check the headlines. She pulled out her wireless ear buds and put the right one in her ear, then pulled up her news aggregator app.

'What am I seeing here?' she asked, her heartbeat raising as she took in the headlines.

FOOTBALL STAR INJURED IN FALL

Her mind raced as she tried to process what she was seeing.

'A tragic accident. Happened just after you left. Quite the tumble he took. Both legs broken in several places. For a player at this point in his career, it's a death sentence.'

Annabel was certain Ousman's choice of words was deliberate. She was certain the accident had something to do with him. She felt terrible. She had put Emmanuel in danger. But there was more at play. She didn't want anyone to be a victim, but a millionaire's broken leg was a drop in the ocean compared to the pain suffered by the thousands of victims lured from their homes to take treacherous journeys to foreign lands, only to be press-ganged into modern slavery and prostitution.

'Ms. Green?' She had been wrapped up in her thoughts for too long. 'I hope I'm coming through clearly? It has been a long time since a journalist has disappeared in Europe, but it still can happen. And I happen to know some excellent magicians.'

The line went dead. Annabel looked outside. It was raining. She fetched her umbrella from her bag and stepped out onto the street.

As she contemplated whether to walk or hail a cab, out of the corner of her eye she saw a black shape speed from her left. The van stopped abruptly and the side door swung open in one seamless motion. Men, Annabel couldn't count how many, emerged from the vehicle, moving towards her. Annabel's brain couldn't compute what was happening. Her eyes widened as two men — dressed all in black, balaclavas pulled down over their faces — grabbed her arms.

Annabel couldn't find the strength to struggle when a third man approached, pulled a black cloth sack over her head and dragged her into the rear of the van. It felt as though she was under water, her limbs weighed down with lead weights. She was sinking. She didn't feel the blow to the side of her head, but saw her vision fuzz over, black spots floating in front of her eyes. She heard her breath, heavy and laboured. Felt a thud against her ribs. The ground rushing up towards her as she lost strength in her arms and the blackness descended on her as she sank into oblivion.

19

The first thing Afam noticed was the sharp pain that sat right behind his eyes. He kept them closed, knowing instinctively that any contact with light would send pain shooting through his head. He tried to focus on something, anything, else. Traffic noise made its way through to his ears, the roll of rubber against tarmac. It sounded as though he was in the back of a truck. Memories flooded back to his travels from Lagos to Tripoli, pressed against the others, everyone trying desperately not to move, trying to stave off the cramp that came through being stuck inside a crate whilst they made their way through border checkpoints.

The memory brought his thoughts into sharp focus. He needed to stay vigilant. He opened his eyes and was met with pitch black. What was happening? He remembered the blow to the side of his head. Had it done something to his eyes? He forced himself to calm, slowing his breathing. He felt the warmth of his breath blow back onto his skin, the rough feeling of fabric against his lips.

'Hello?' he called out.

Silence.

'Leye? What are you doing man? Take this thing off my head.' It was coming back to him now.

Silence again, until: 'Afam?' A woman's voice, not Leye's.

'Annabel?' Afam's voice croaked, his throat parched like he'd been sleeping with his mouth open. He tried to work up some saliva and made to speak out again.

'Annab—' Someone cuffed him on the side of the head. It felt a little like the correcting hand of his mother. Not hard, but hard enough to know you had to stop whatever you were doing.

'Keep your mouth shut, Afam. It's for the best,' Leye insisted.

'Where am I?' Afam continued, 'What are you doing? Where are you taking us?'

More silence.

'You should have stayed quiet, Afam,' Isaac spoke up now, 'It would have been so much easier for you. Should've left the journalist alone. But now you've seen what we do, and I've seen what you do. You're a snitch, Afam. A rat. Rats are vermin, only one thing for them. Such a shame, you could've ended up earning a little bit on the side. You just had to keep your mouth shut, pay up, and live out the rest of your days. Who knows, one day maybe you'd have made it back home. Should've listened to Leye. That kid knows his place. He'll go far. Well,' Isaac laughed, 'Further than you, at least.'

They continued to drive and Afam realised how ridiculous it was in movies when the hero guessed which way they were going from a car boot. He was completely disoriented, the only thing he knew was that it was the back of the black van that he'd willingly entered.

'You won't get away with this.' Afam heard Annabel say. Her voice was muffled, and he guessed she had also had a sack pulled down over her head. 'Nothing I'm doing here is under the radar. My bosses know exactly where I am. Where I'm supposed to be. If I don't check in with them in a few days, they'll come looking. And they're well connected. Much better than a few corner boys could ever be. You'll burn.'

'Watch out boys,' Isaac chuckled, 'She's a live one! Please,' he directed this at Annabel now, 'By the time anyone figures out you're not here we'll all be long gone. Anyway, you've been poking your nose into the business of some powerful people. Ousman might look like a fool, but he's not a guy to cross. You're right, he's way more powerful than I'll ever be... but who cares? Do I want his stress? He's paying me to shut you up and then I get to go home. Pepin, and Félix and the other guys at The Table will make sure nothing comes back to me, or to them. Easy day's work.'

Annabel went quiet. She couldn't see a way out of this. She hadn't even begun to suspect that The Table could be involved in this, but it made complete sense. Their tendrils reached into all corners of the football world, it made complete sense that they'd have contacts at top organisations, in government. Anything that happened to her and Afam would be swept under the carpet and if it did ever come out, the people who wanted to silence her had layers upon layers of plausible deniability. Not even Isaac would take the rap. In the unlikely event that the authorities caught onto anything, it would be passed down the chain of command to some foot soldier who would get a cash bonus for taking the heat, and the badge of honour that came with doing a stretch of time. Perhaps it wouldn't even be one of the gang, but someone in the same position as Afam found himself, taking the blame in exchange for their family's safety back home.

The van slowed down, its tyres crunching on gravel and dirt. They had come off the main road. The van lurched forwards as they came to a halt, throwing Afam against the body sat next to him. Afam traced the sounds, trying to build a picture of what was happening with the only sense he could trust at that moment. The click of seat belts disengaging, followed by the heavy clunk and thud of doors at the front of the van being opened and closed. It briefly amazed Afam at how attuned his hearing had become as he traced footsteps along the side of the van. Light poured into the back of the van as the rear doors slid open and Afam was unceremoniously hoisted up and bundled out.

Afam fell as his feet touched the ground. His hands had been bound, so he had no way to break his fall. The ground rushed up to meet him, knocking the wind out of his lungs. His forehead hit the ground, adding to the pain that still hadn't disappeared. Hands dragged him back up and shoved him forward, and he had to work hard to stay on his feet. He looked down and could see the briefest sliver of dusty scrub through a gap in his hood, which helped him situate himself. No doubt they had taken them away from the city.

A sharp kick hit the back of Afam's knee and he went down. He caught himself half-way down and managed to remain on one knee but another kick came, a shove with the sole of a foot, forcing him down to the ground, his bound hands again offering no opportunity to break his fall. He was grateful this time for the hood, which stopped him eating a mouthful of dirt.

Afam's hood was pulled off violently as they lifted him back up to his knees. He sat back on his heels, squinting against the light, violently bright despite the setting sun. Shapes began to emerge out of the blinding white as Afam looked around at his surroundings. They were in some sort of industrial estate. Rows of towering corrugated iron buildings stretched off into the distance, roll-down shutters closed for the evening. It was silent, save for the distant hum of motorway traffic. Several people stood in front of him, leaning against a black mass he presumed was the van they'd been travelling in. He screwed his eyes shut and when he opened them again, Isaac was in front of him, close enough that Afam could smell the coffee on his breath mingling with the harsh, acrid smell of tobacco.

'So, Superstar, what are you going to do now?'

At this, the collected bodies began to laugh. Afam sensed a struggle and turned his head. Annabel was not making it easy for them to get her out of the van. She kicked out and threw her head at Skinny and Leye, who were trying to grab hold of her arms.

'Get the fuck off of m—' Her yell was cut short as Skinny, having had enough climbed back inside the van and pushed her out of the door, sending her flying down the step. Leye tried to break her fall, but she landed with a heavy thud. Afam watched as Skinny jumped down after her and he and Leye scooped Annabel up, dragging her over to sit in front of Afam. Her hood was whipped off and Afam stared as Annabel squinted in the sudden brightness of the light. Her makeup had run, dark streaks of mascara smearing under her eyes, and a small cut on her eyebrow was bleeding down the side of her face. Annabel scrunched up her eyes, trying to correct her vision, and to scratch the itch the bead of blood was causing as it coursed across her cheekbone.

The sound of Isaac laughing again brought everything into sharp focus.

'My god, she really is a fighter. Won't do you any good out here, miss, but I'm impressed.'

Annabel spat on the ground next to her.

'What are you doing this for? What do you get out of this?'

'Honestly?' Isaac answered, 'The money's okay, and having friends in high places has its obvious benefits... but really and truly?' he paused, tense silence filling the air, 'I enjoy it.' At this, a grin spread across his face.

Annabel glanced at Afam and for the first time he saw genuine fear in her eyes. Tears began to form, but she quickly blinked them away, not wanting to give her captors — her executioners — the satisfaction. Afam tried to hold her gaze as Isaac stalked a circle around them, gun now hanging easily at his side.

The whole world seemed to zone out to Afam and all he could hear was his own breath, the faint crunch of gravel beneath Isaac's feet. Afam maintained eye contact with Annabel. Isaac stopped behind her. Annabel closed her eyes, her head bowing forward involuntarily. Afam tried to catch her eye again, but her head stayed down. Afam heard her breathing slow down, moving steadily in and out of her body which rose and fell with each lungful.

'This is the part,' Isaac said, 'Where you're supposed to give us your last words. But they're always so boring. 'Fuck you...' is about the best they ever get. Let's get this straight, I'm not passing on any messages to your dearly beloved.'

'Fuck you.'

Afam heard the click of the hammer being cocked back, saw Annabel's breath catch. Before he could figure out what was happening, Afam had jumped up from his kneeling position, almost involuntarily, his body screaming for survival. He drove his head into the underneath of Isaac's chin, sparking him out cold, sending him and his weapon flailing.

Before the others had a chance to respond, Afam was on his feet, sprinting at full pace towards them, screaming at the top of his lungs. Like rabbits in headlights they all froze, trying to process what had just happened, the shock of everything causing microsecond delays. But that was all Afam needed. He lunged at Skinny, throwing his shoulder into the man's stomach, crashing him into the side of the van.

'Run!' he yelled back to Annabel, 'Annabel, get up, go! Run!'

It took Annabel a few seconds to figure out what was happening, but as she came back to reality she jumped up to her feet. And ran.

20

Annabel ran.

Her hands were bound in front of her but she swung her body as she moved, urging herself forward faster. She had a good head start on Isaac and his men, but the further she ran, the slower she could feel herself getting. She had not picked a particular direction when she had bolted, had just followed wherever her legs had taken her.

Annabel had made several random turns, staying away from the main roads in and out of the vast industrial area in an effort to confuse her pursuers. She checked behind her and seeing that there was nobody within her line of sight, slowed down, taking refuge behind a large industrial bin. She sucked in large gulps of air, replenishing her aching muscles with the oxygen they needed. As Annabel controlled her breath, she gained a little mental clarity.

Annabel had put enough distance between herself and the men who had taken them. She needed to think, to come up with a plan, a way to get to safety. She needed to keep up the pace, but if she stuck to the shadows that had begun to descend on the estate, she could be smarter, could increase her situational awareness. Years ago, Annabel had run a story on an all-female football team in Afghanistan. She'd gone to the Brecon Beacons for a weekend to take part in some tactical training about safety and survival in a combat zone. Three days of being woken up by screaming ex-Special Forces officers — though she had never been entirely confident how 'ex' they were — and being forced into all sorts of uncomfortable situations in the freezing Welsh countryside. She'd failed to see at the time how the skills she had learned in the near-constant drizzle and wind could translate to the arid deserts of Afghanistan, and of course she had never had even the slightest reason to use anything she had learned when she was in-country. But she was glad of it now. Glad she was able to think clearly, to assess the situation, to make a plan.

One thing she couldn't account for was Afam. She had no idea what had happened to him. One moment she had been bent on her knees, steadying herself, making peace with her fate and the next there had been an explosion of violence. Afam had hurled himself into her would-be executioner, had told her to run. Part of her had wanted to stay, to help, but she knew that she would be no use to Afam with her hands bound. All she could do was run, so run she had. What would be the use of his sacrifice if she'd been caught too? A thought struck her. She had heard no gunfire as she'd escaped. Could Afam have survived his kamikaze assault? If nothing else, this confirmed that he was not merely the victim of a scam football academy as he'd told her. He was into things a lot deeper. And the guy, Isaac, had mentioned Pepin and Félix by name. If they got out of here alive, the story she would write would be explosive.

Annabel scanned the ground around the bin, but not finding what she wanted she hoisted herself back to standing and clumsily opened the lid. The hot, sweet smell of accumulated trash hit her full force, and she gagged. She searched the top of the bin until she found what she was looking for. Glass. Annabel reached her bound hands up and inside the bin — they had been tied in front of her — stretching herself out, but the bottle she was reaching for was too far out of reach. She placed a foot on the wheel of the bin and levered herself up with her arms, inching herself closer and closer. Her fingertips grazed the bottom of the bottle, but in her excitement she attempted to grab it and sent it further into the skip. Annabel controlled her breathing, tamped down the adrenaline that was surging through her. One foot on the wheel, she smeared her other on the side of the bin and hurled herself inside. The landing was soft. She gagged again as the smell came at her in full force and she felt something seeping through her clothes. She had twisted to land on her back, so moved onto her stomach and crawled towards the elusive bottle. Clasping it firmly with both hands, she smashed it against the side of the container. It took several attempts to break, each whack on the sheet metal seemed as loud as a grenade, but Annabel was eventually left holding the jagged remains of the bottleneck. Carefully, she turned the neck around and jammed it between her knees. A sharp point dug into her skin but she ignored the pain for now as she began sawing at the plastic zip ties that had bound her wrists.

As she set about her work, Annabel opened her ears to the world around her. Still quiet, though she heard the distant noise of men shouting and several doors opening and slamming shut. Still no gunshots. That had to be good. Had to mean Afam had escaped as well. She clung onto that hope. It also meant they were coming for her now. She focused back on the bindings tightened cruelly around her wrist. When she was about half way through the plastic, Annabel yanked hard and the bindings separated. Freedom. Now she just had to find Afam and get the two of them back to Paris.

***

Afam's arm hurt. He had landed hard when he had tackled Isaac and again when he'd barrelled Skinny into the van. Leye had made a half-hearted attempt to grab him, but Afam had taken advantage of the confusion he'd caused and sprinted off in the opposite direction to Annabel. The guys had been too focused on Isaac, unconscious on the floor, and had taken their attention off of Afam. He had run like he'd never run before, grateful for the training he'd put in over the last season.

Confident he'd put enough distance between them, Afam slowed to a jog. He needed to keep moving. The sun had set, finally, and the darkness of the shadows cast by the surrounding buildings offered a decent amount of cover. He just needed to avoid the floodlights that lit up the primary routes through the industrial area. And he needed to get his hands free, in case he had to run again.

Afam turned down a gap between two buildings, looking for something sharp but couldn't find anything. The estate was surprisingly well maintained. Save for a few stray scraps of paper and a plastic Carrefour shopping bag, the floor was deserted. He reached the end of the alley between the two warehouse buildings and realised he'd come to a dead end. The path was closed off at one end by a rusty metal panelled fence that looked as though it had been green at one point in its life. He leaned against the fence, thinking of his next move. Isaac, Skinny and Leye would likely have got themselves together now. They'd be back in the van, back searching for him. Searching for her.

Afam shifted his body weight forward, and the fence groaned behind him, the squeal of metal sparking an idea. He turned to see that one of the fence panels was loose, exposing the thin metal where two panels met. He sawed at his wrist binding and before too long the plastic had snapped. His hands were free. He rubbed his arm. It still hurt from where he had fallen, closed his eyes and listened to the night. A noise in the distance, like the beating of a large drum, followed by the shatter of glass. A few moments later, an engine roared to life. Afam ran again. This time, towards the noise.

* * *

Annabel was crouched around the corner of one of the large warehouses. There was the unmistakable odour of engine grease, the remnants of an oil spill in the area immediately in front of the building. Cat litter sprinkled liberally all over it. She watched the yard ahead of her as the black van that had brought them all here crawled along the road. Its headlights were switched to full-beam and cast a wide glare over the surrounding buildings.

The van crawled around the yard, heading towards Annabel and she ducked her head back around the corner. She listened to the low timbre of the engine, the high-pitched suck of the rubber against the tarmac as the van came closer. The lights picked out everything around her, casting harsh chiaroscuro across the forecourt, silhouetting the odd assortment of shapes against the bare walls of the surrounding buildings. Annabel held her breath as the van rolled past, tucked herself in as tight as she could against the side of the building, ensuring she was hidden behind the boxes she had collected around herself at her vantage point. She saw a man's face squinting out of the window; not Isaac, one of his men. The one that Afam seemed to know. Had he called him Leye? He was scanning every inch of the area. She watched as the van rolled past, and the tension in her body released as the rear lights came into view. They would carry on looking, of course, but at least now she had some sense of where they were. It would be easier to stay out of their way.

Annabel struggled to scream as a hand clamped over her mouth. An arm wrapped round her shoulder, clamping her tight. She struggled, but it was useless. Whoever had hold of her was strong. Of course it had been too good to be true. The van had been bait, had lured her into a false sense of security.

'Shh,' a voice whispered harshly in her ear, 'Keep quiet, Annabel.' She kicked back, her heel connecting with shinbone, but the grip held.

'Ah!' the voice said, 'Please, Annabel, it's me Afam.'

Afam felt Annabel relax and released his grip. 'Sorry, I didn't want to scare you, but I couldn't risk you running.'

The slap was hard, full strength. It set his ears ringing, which Afam was temporarily glad of, given the berating he was now at the receiving end of.

'Are you fucking insane? Who in the living fuck raised you? How on God's green Earth did you think this was the best approach?' Annabel was wild-eyed, Afam stayed wary in case another slap was forthcoming. Annabel twisted away from Afam and doubled over, hands on knees, catching her breath. After a few moments, Afam tried again to explain.

'Anna—'

'Just... don't. It's okay, I'm sorry I slapped you. You're a fucking idiot, you deserved it, but I'm still sorry. Thanks for coming back for me.'

'Coming back? I never left. I've been wandering around this place for ages trying to find you. It's like a maze. Everything looks exactly the same. Exactly.'

'I know, right? Anyway, look, the van headed that way. I know enough French to know that,' she pointed at some yellow markings on the floor reading SORTIE in block capitals, 'Means 'exit'. Stick to the shadows, follow me. We need to get back to the city.'

21

Annabel and Afam had eventually found their way to the exit of the industrial estate. The road outside only led one way and so they had trudged along the side of the road. It was slow going as they stuck as close as possible to the hedgerow that lined the road, ready to take cover should they see a vehicle approach. Nothing came though, and eventually they found themselves on a major road which had its share of night time traffic. Despite having lived in a city her entire life, it never failed to amaze Annabel when roads were busy in the dead of night. Dawn commuters she could understand, but where were so many people going at two in the morning?

They walked for several miles, following road signs pointing back to Paris, cowering at the prospect of the twenty-kilometre walk they were facing. They walked with their arms outstretched, thumbs cocked, in the blind hope that someone would stop for them. Thunder rumbled in the distance and rain began to spatter down on the two hitchhikers.

'So what's your deal really, Afam?' Annabel asked. She turned to face him and was immediately jealous of the hood he had pulled up against the brunt of the weather. His eyes were bloodshot, heavy bags puffed out from underneath. His skin was grey and dry, lips cracked and parched. Far away from the bright young man she'd first met.

'My deal?'

'Come on, Afam, I think we can do away with the cover story can't we? It's clear there's more to all of this than what you originally told me... Tell me, Afam. What really happened? Tell me everything.'

So he did.

* * *

'Afam, I am so sorry,' Annabel said. They were walking side by side, not particularly focused on getting back to the city quickly any more. Annabel had listened intently as Afam had spilled the truth about his plight. About Samuel's death, their escape out of Lagos, crossing the water and then Afam's horrific start to being in Paris. Annabel had barely spoken the whole time, but she had listened intently, taking it in, feeling every word.

'Does Moussa know?' she asked.

'I've never told him,' Afam said, 'But I don't think he believes what I did tell him. When you've seen as much as Moussa has, you get good at seeing the holes in a story.'

'He's definitely seen a lot,' said Annabel, smiling at the thought of her old acquaintance, and of the good he kept trying to make of the world. She looked off into the distance for a few moments. 'I think you should tell him.'

'What? Why?' Afam said, 'If he finds out I lied to him, he'll never trust me again.'

'Come on, Afam, some lies are necessary. You know that... Moussa will understand. And we need to tell your story, Afam. It's the thing that ties together everything I've been looking into. This isn't just organisations looking the other way whilst knowing this sort of stuff is going on. They're actively involved in it. They're facilitating human trafficking. The closer I get to this, the more they try to keep me away. You heard what Isaac said back there. His orders came from higher up the chain of command. You have to be on a fairly high rung to be able to order a gangland execution without fear of repercussion. This goes beyond Georges Pepin, beyond Ousman.'

'Who are they?'

'Pepin is some low-rent Sepp Blatter. One of my contacts had me look into him, she was sure he was involved in trafficking kids over to France, but the more I looked, the more I realised he's just a patsy. A distraction. I don't need to tell you about all the fake academies in Africa. Well, Pepin was facilitating these dodgy academies, making sure no one looked too close, and getting paid under the table for doing it. But he's an idiot, walking around in new suits, flashing expensive watches, high-end sports cars. But the stuff he was involved in was a drop in the ocean. Ousman, Isaac and that crew, they were keeping Pepin in line, providing him with a bit of a scare now and then... but really, they were going over Pepin's head and working directly with his paymasters. With everyone looking at Georges, no one was looking any higher up the chain.'

Afam shook his head in disbelief. He was finding it difficult to join the dots, but Annabel seemed to know what she was talking about so he stayed quiet.

Afam and Annabel had all but given up on their hitchhiking attempt, and had resigned themselves to walking back into Paris. Eventually, though, a work van pulled up alongside them, high-vis stripes indicating it was some sort of highway maintenance team.

After an awkward, stilted conversation, they eventually managed to convince the driver and his mate to give them a ride into Paris. The middle-aged driver keeping a constant, wary eye on Afam. Understanding the limits of their language skills, the four rode back into Paris in complete silence, the only noise the bubbling suck of the apprentice's vape pen as he billowed vapour into the cab at an alarming rate. Annabel closed her eyes, finding some small comfort in the candy-floss haze, and daydreamed of trips to the funfair on Finsbury Park as a child.

She was pulled out of her doze by Afam gently shaking her shoulder.

'Annabel,' he said, 'I think we're back.'

She opened her eyes and saw the city skyline rising up ahead of her, the historic architecture butting up against the contemporary steel and glass monoliths, both set in stark contrast against the plain concrete functionality of the conference centres and graffiti-tagged slip roads that encircled the city.

'*Où dois-je te déposer?*' The driver spoke up for the first time since he'd picked them up.

Annabel turned to Afam, the awkward look on her face carrying the inherent embarrassment of a generation of English people with the financial and political freedom to travel the world, failed by a post-Imperial education system that didn't see the need for its students to learn foreign languages.

'Where are we going?' Afam asked Annabel.

'Let's go back to my hotel first — I need to charge my phone, grab a few things. And I think we could both do with a shower,' Annabel replied. 'Could you ask him to drop us off?'

Afam tapped the driver on the shoulder. 'Pourriez-vous nous emmener près du neuvième arrondissement?'

'*S'il vous plaît?*' Annabel added.

The driver turned to her, his eyes wide as he feigned a massive shock, which soon turned to a warm, generous smile.

'*Oui, madame,*' he replied, and then in heavily accented English, 'Of course.'

They pulled up outside Annabel's hotel. Pierre, the driver, had insisted on dropping them off at the door. They had made their goodbyes and headed up to Annabel's room.

'You live like this?' Afam said, shocked at the chaos of Annabel's room.

'I'm a busy person,' she replied, defensively, 'I literally don't have the time to put stuff away.'

'Seriously? I have a job, training, and live in an attic and it's cleaner than this. Do they not have room service or something? Someone who comes in and tidies up?'

'They do,' Annabel replied, her hackles still raised, 'But I put up the sign. I don't like people clearing up after me. It's not fair. It's my mess, I'll tidy it. Eventually. Now, are you just going to stand there all day being rude or are you going to get ready?'

She picked up a towel from the floor and threw it at Afam. He brought it to his nose, sniffed, and shrugged. It would do.

'Bathroom's over there,' Annabel pointed to the small en-suite by the door, 'Help yourself to anything you need. I don't have a spare toothbrush, you'll have to borrow mine. Gross, I know, but better than bad breath.'

Afam made his way to the bathroom and shut the door behind him. Annabel heard the water being turned on and started packing a bag, throwing in clothes and underwear without a second thought. She grabbed her laptop off of the bureau in the corner of the room, bundling up the assortment of charging cables and power banks and throwing it on top of the garments, then zipped up the bag. Lastly she went to the safe and retrieved her emergency cash and her passport. She would need to be in touch with Larry, her editor, to explain what had happened. He would be able to help. They needed to get Afam out of the country, away from the danger he had helped her escape.

The water from the shower cut out and Afam emerged holding a bundle of clothes.

'I don't suppose you've got a change of clothes for me?'

Annabel thought for a moment. 'As a matter of fact, you're in luck,' she scanned the floor next to the bed and picked up a man's t-shirt. 'It's not completely clean, but it's better than what you've got on — I just sleep in it.'

Afam pulled on the shirt, which felt a little snug under his armpits, held out his arms and gave a twirl.

'It'll do. We'll get back to yours and you can grab some stuff. I'm going to need to speak to a few people. I think we need to get you out of here. Maybe I can bring you back with me to the UK.'

'But Annabel,' Afam said, resignation in his voice, 'They took my passport. I can't leave without that.'

'Well, let's see what we can do about that. Come on, get dressed.'

* * *

The Uber was waiting for them outside the hotel as they exited the lobby. Annabel and Afam got in the back of the car and instructed the driver where to go. As soon as they'd set off, Annabel pulled out her phone.

'Sorry,' she said, 'I've got a few things to do if this is going to work.'

'Not a problem,' Afam said, and leaned his head against the rear window. He watched as Paris streets rolled by, vaguely remembering some of the buildings they passed on the way from the last time he had been in this corner of the city. The first time he had met Isaac. The thought of Isaac and his cronies caused panic to rise in Afam's chest. They would still be looking for them. Surely they would have someone watching the house. He shifted uncomfortably in his seat, something was digging into his back. He unzipped his jacket pocket and his hand touched cold, hard, steel. The gun. He had completely forgotten about it. Leye. If they couldn't find Afam, what would they do to him? He was too close to them. Afam had to find him, warn him. A last act of friendship.

22

'Hello?' Afam called out as he opened the front door to the house he shared with his friends. No response. They would all be at training. Afam let Annabel in behind him.

'Wait here,' he said, as he climbed the stairs, 'I'll just be a few minutes.' Annabel sat on the bottom step of the staircase and pulled out her phone. She was sending emails to everyone she trusted; Moussa, David, Jim her editor, a lawyer contact she had, and someone at Amnesty. She had to find a way to get Afam safely out of the country. It was the only way they would both be safe.

True to his word, Afam returned less than ten minutes later, taking the stairs two at a time. He had put on clean clothes and had a rucksack slung over his shoulder. There seemed to be a spring in his step, which elevated Annabel's mood.

'Right,' Annabel said, 'Ready?' She put the copy of GQ she had been flicking through back onto the occasional table next to her and looked into the mirror on the wall, pulling her hair into a tight bun.

'Wait, Annabel, before we go there's one more thing.'

'Hm, yes what is it?' Annabel stood up and Afam reached into his rucksack. He pulled out the gun he had found in Leye's bed.

Annabel recoiled. 'What the fuck is that, Afam?' Annabel asked. After her encounter with Isaac she never wanted to see another gun in her life.

'Relax!' Afam said, 'Please relax. It's not mine. I found it in my room when I was throwing out all of Leye's stuff. He's in deep, Annabel. I need to help him, I think. The Leye who would keep this gun is not the person I know. He's good in his heart. But I know the sorts of pressure these people can put on you.'

'Afam, that's as may be, but why are you showing it to me?'

'I don't know,' Afam said, feeling embarrassed, 'I just thought you might know what to do with it.'

Annabel sighed and closed her eyes.

'Come on,' she said, 'Let's go.'

Afam tucked the gun into his waistband and they left the house, locking the door behind them.

'So,' Afam asked, as they headed away from the house back towards the city, 'Where are we actually going?'

'I've not quite figured that out yet, but let's head back into town. I need to make a few calls, so do you mind if we walk? I need a bit of time.'

'Of course. Come on, they've closed off the street up there, it's best to cut through here.'

They slipped down an alleyway between two buildings, Annabel falling behind as she navigated her phone. Afam was a few paces ahead when he heard a loud crack behind him, a whimper, and the slump of a body. He turned and saw Annabel crumpled on the ground, arms and legs splayed out. A man stood over her, breathing heavily.

'Leye?'

Leye looked like he hadn't slept since Afam had seen him yesterday. His clothes were crumpled and stained, his eyes were bloodshot — from lack of sleep or drink or narcotics, Afam couldn't tell. Perhaps all three. He imagined that Isaac hadn't let them relent in their search for him and Annabel. He stared at Afam, wild-eyed, barely focusing as he stared down the barrel of the handgun he held out in front of him.

'I'm sorry,' Leye said, finally, his voice strained as he choked out the words, 'I didn't want it to come to this. I told you to steer clear of this lady, Afam. She's bad news, has a lot of people who want her to keep quiet. She's a troublemaker, Afam. You think she cares about you? You're going against your countrymen, your friends, your family, to help her out. You can still come work for them, Afam; I spoke to Isaac, he said he can put everything behind him, if you come do the work you promised him you'd do. Earn some money, Afam, keep your family safe.'

'She doesn't care about me? Are you crazy?' Afam was struggling to keep his anger contained. He wanted to reach out to Leye, to make him see sense. Shouting wasn't going to achieve that. 'You think that Isaac cares about you? He's using you, Leye. He used you to find me, try to recruit me, and now he's using you to do his dirty work. You accuse me of going against my people — what about Isaac? What about you? You're holding a gun to the head of a fellow Nigerian. Another illegal immigrant. A brother. Another victim, same as you. We should be working together to stop people like Isaac doing this to anyone else. With the stuff that Annabel's been looking into we might have a chance to do that — to stop anyone else getting hurt. That's why I'm working with her.'

'You think we can ever be safe now? As soon as you chop off one head, three more emerge. How can you not see that? If you can't beat them, join them, Afam.'

Afam barely recognised the friend he had known back in AJ City. Leye had always skirted the fringes of the law, had always had one foot in the door with the wrong crowd. But he was a good kid, a good friend. He was a part of Afam's family.

'Give me the gun, Leye,' Afam was firm now, serious. He was staring into Leye's face, but out of the corner of his eye he saw movement from Annabel. Leye hadn't noticed. At first her leg twitched, then, like a corpse reanimating, she came back to life — regaining mobility as her consciousness snapped back into action.

Afam tried to maintain eye contact with Leye as Annabel got to her feet. He kept talking to keep his attention.

'Leye, the gun. Come on. It's me, Afam. Just put it on the ground and come with us. Think about home, Leye. Think about your mother. My mother. Iman. Our families. They would hate to see you like this, Leye. You've fallen a long way, but it's okay. We can get through this. Together. Me, you, and Annabel.'

As he said her name, his eyes inadvertently flicked behind Leye to where Annabel was. She crept around to Leye's flank, treading carefully so as not to make a sound. The floor was littered with empty, half-broken bottles and crushed cans. Desperate not to draw attention to her, Afam returned his gaze to a still silent Leye. Tears welled up in Leye's bloodshot eyes, rolling down his face. Afam took a step towards him, arms outstretched placatingly. Leye started at the movement, snapping his arm back up, bringing the gun to bear on Afam once more. Afam stopped.

'There's nothing we can do, Afam. You talk about our mothers, your sisters, brothers, my family — well, they know where they are, Afam. All it would take is one phone call and their threats become reality. There's too much riding on all of this — what do they care about knocking a few heads along the way? I know these people, Afam. They wouldn't hesitate. Come, please. Help me. Help them. Do as they say.'

A movement caught Afam's eye and once again he flickered his gaze to Annabel, just a few paces behind Leye. This time Leye noticed. He snapped around, gun raised, but Annabel was on him, leaping like a wildcat at his central mass. Leye staggered, and the gun knocked out of his hand, skidding across the pavement. Afam was frozen in place as he watched Leye and Annabel scrabble around on the pavement in front of him. With the element of surprise gone, Leye was beginning to overpower Annabel.

Leye shoved Annabel away from him as she flailed her arms and legs, slamming against the wall of the alley and slumping down into a pile of refuse sacks that split, spilling their putrid contents across the floor. Leye turned and stooped down for the gun, shifting his weight back round and taking aim at Annabel.

'No!' Afam unfroze, launching himself at Leye, pushing the arm wielding the weapon up into the sky. A shot rang out, reverberating off of the walls of the alleyway, the noise amplified into a violent crack that felt like it popped Afam's ear-drums. He instinctively brought a finger up to his ear and shook it around to clear the ringing. He grabbed Leye's arm with his free hand and brought it crashing down on the rung of a fire-escape ladder that ran down the side of one of the buildings. The weapon clattered to the floor and Afam kicked it mightily, sending it skittering away out of sight.

Then Leye was on him, landing solid punches to Afam's ribs, knocking the wind out of him. Instinct took over and suddenly Leye wasn't his friend, he was only a threat. A threat that had to be put down so that he and Annabel could escape. He shoved Leye away, getting some distance between them, which allowed him to land a few body blows on Leye. He felt his hand connect with the soft belly underneath Leye's ribs and Leye doubled over, sucking air through gritted teeth. Afam brought his leg up and threw the sole of his foot towards Leye's rib cage, sending him sprawling.

'Leye, enough,' Afam said, panting, 'If you don't want to go, fine, but let us go.' He walked over to Leye, still prone on the ground, and held out a conciliatory hand. Leye turned onto his back and stared at Afam, blood from a graze above his right eye mingling with the sheen of perspiration that covered his face. His eyes bore into Afam's as he looked up at his friend. His breathing slowed as he brought it under control. He took a deep breath and held out his hand, which Afam grabbed tightly. As he made to bring his friend to his feet, Afam was thrown off balance as Leye pulled him down into the dirt with him. Afam landed hard on his hip and heard the unmistakable clatter of metal on the pavement. The gun. The one he had found in Leye's bed. He had kept it tucked in his waistband this whole time.

As Afam lay wincing from the pain in his hip, Leye scrambled to his feet and launched towards the gun. Afam flung out an arm, grabbing him by the ankle, sending him sprawling again. But he had his hand on the gun. He grabbed it firmly and swung the barrel around. Afam intercepted the arc, then brought himself in close to Leye, wrapping him in a bear hug, making it impossible for Leye to get off a shot.

Annabel was back up on her feet again. It felt as though she had been watching the two boys fight for years, but in reality it was less than two minutes. Seeing the gun in Leye's hand she launched straight forward, grabbing at his wrist trying to shake it free.

But Leye held on, jostling his two assailants, twisting and turning himself away so as not to lose his grip on the firearm. He twisted his gun-arm free of Afam's bear hug and brought the weapon up to point at his friend's stomach. A moment's hesitation and Annabel wrenched his wrist away from Afam's central mass. A shot rang out. The three froze, time standing still as the sound of the shot reverberated once more off of the walls of the buildings, ping-ponging between the surfaces out into the open sky above. Two gunshots. Even in a run-down area like this, the police would be here soon.

Afam and Leye stared at one another, each one shocked out of their fight by the sound of the gun going off.

Still wrapped in his embrace, Afam felt Leye grow heavy, saw his eyes widen in horror. Afam took the brunt of Leye's weight, helping him down to the ground. Leye moved a hand to his stomach and felt the wetness that was spreading there. Brought his hand up to his face and saw the blood covering his fingertips. His breathing rate increased as panic set in.

'Shit... Shit!' Annabel screamed, digging around in her bag and pulling out her phone and dialling the emergency services number.

'Leye, it's going to be okay,' Afam said, doing his best to remain calm so as not to further panic his friend, 'Annabel's calling the ambulance now. I think the police might be on their way as well — someone's bound to have heard those gunshots.'

'No. Police,' Leye struggled to get the words out, wincing and groaning through the pain.

'Come on, Leye — that time has passed. We need to get you help.' Afam was trying to stay calm, but he had never seen so much blood.

'If they find out,' Leye's speech was stilted, his breathing laboured, 'They'll kill me. They'll think that I snitched. I never would.' Suddenly he doubled up, writhing against the pain. 'I don't want to die here, Afam. I want to die at home.'

'Don't be stupid, man — you're not going to die.' He looked over to Annabel, who he could hear struggling to explain their location.

Leye let out another animalistic groan and rolled over onto his side. Afam ran over to where he'd dropped his rucksack and pulled out a bundle of spare clothes. He charged back to Leye's side and pulled up his shirt. Given how much had soaked through to Leye's clothes, Afam had expected to see blood gushing out of a gaping wound in his friend's stomach. But the hole the bullet had left looked fairly neat, and the blood pulsed softly in time with Leye's heartbeat. There was a livid bruise spreading from the hole and Leye's whole abdomen had started to swell.

Afam bunched up one of the t-shirts he had grabbed from his bag and pressed it firmly against the wound. Leye blew hard through pursed lips, but Afam kept the pressure on the wound.

'Afam,' Leye spoke through the pain, 'I'm sorry. Please, tell Iman I'm sorry. I put you all in danger.'

'It wasn't you, Leye. It was Isaac, it was all those guys back home. And if Annabel's right, this goes a lot deeper than them all. The moment we approached them we were playing a rigged game. Nothing we could do. Not even you. Don't worry. We're going to get through this. We're going to help Annabel. And we're going to go home. We're going to make everything right.'

'But... I've been working with them. No,' he stopped Afam's attempt to interject, 'More than just foot soldier work. I found you for them. And I've been watching you.'

Afam stopped in his tracks.

'It wasn't easy,' Leye continued, 'I was in the middle of nowhere, hiding out from my cousin's boss. A couple of the guys found out where I was and came to me, said they were going to rat me out unless I helped them. They'd heard from some friends in Paris that some kid who they'd trafficked had made a little good. They wanted a piece of the action, but their boys in Paris — Isaac — didn't want to scare him off. Didn't want to scare you off. They needed information.' Leye winced. 'I told them about Iman.'

'What? You did what? You put my sister in danger? She told me. They've been following her home from school. Waiting outside the house. I can't believe this. How could you?'

'I'm sorry, Afam, I'm sorry. But once they knew about her, I had to keep going to stop her getting hurt.' Tears had started to fall from Leye's eyes, 'So I found you. I talked to people back home and pieced everything together. It was tough. There are millions of people here, Afam. But I found you. And then I watched you. I watched you go to work. Watched you train. I kept trying to throw them off the scent, but they knew I had you. They wanted me to get back in with you so I could stay close. They wanted a piece of you for the rest of your life and I agreed to give it to them.'

The sounds of sirens wailed in the distance.

'They'll come for you, Afam. They've done it a thousand times before. They wanted you on that job for them so that whenever they want a piece of you in the future, they can use it against you. They were never interested in extorting that guy — the plan was always to murder him. They knew they could escape the heat, but they needed you to know that they could take it all away from you in a moment. I told them I wouldn't do it any more. That's why they jumped you, Afam. Because I told them I couldn't keep hurting you. They had to take matters into their own hands in the only way they know how.'

'Afam, we've got to go — you don't need to get found here.'

Afam snapped back to reality as Annabel spoke to him. He couldn't believe what Leye had told him, couldn't believe how far his friend had sunk. He looked down at the shirt he was holding against Leye's stomach, now soaked through with blood.

'Go,' Leye said, a cough wracking his whole body, 'I'll be fine. Go.'

Afam took Leye's hands and pressed them on top of the bunched material.

'Here,' he said, quietly, 'Keep the pressure on.' He could feel how weak Leye was.

He stood and turned to Annabel.

'Come on,' he said, 'Back this way.' The two turned back the way they had entered the alleyway, Afam taking one last glance over his shoulder towards his old friend. He stared at Leye, waiting to see his chest heave. Eventually he saw his friend take a deep breath and turned away.

'I can't believe we're just leaving him like that,' he said to Annabel.

'I know, Afam. But it's going to be fine. The ambulance is on its way, and it sounds like the police as well. They'll find him and help him. But if they found you there with him, they'd have found out about your refugee status and you'd end up getting caught up in the system. If that happens, there's no way I can help you. If we keep you out of trouble, though, I think I know someone who might be able to help.'

Annabel locked her phone, which she'd been frantically tapping away at as she spoke, and slipped it inside her jacket.

'Is there a taxi stand round here?' she asked Afam.

'Over this way, back towards the city.'

'Great,' she said, 'I've got someone waiting for us at the station. Quicker we get there, the better.'

They reached the taxi rank and only had to wait a few minutes before a cab pulled up. They got in and Annabel gave the address to the driver. The taxi pulled out of the rank, but the driver slammed on his brakes as an ambulance tore past them, sirens blazing, back towards town. Neither Afam nor Annabel said anything for the brief journey, and when they arrived at the Gare du Nord, Annabel paid the driver and she and Afam got out of the cab without a word. In front of the station entrance a bright bronze-red statue of a winged bear stood open-mouthed, bellowing into the sky, its gossamer body working with the colour as a warning, a reminder of the fragility of life on Earth.

Annabel set off for the terminal and Afam followed close behind, not wanting to let her out of his sight. For her safety, but for his as well. A man in an immaculate suit was approaching her quickly from between the Doric pilasters that adorned the station entrance. Afam grabbed Annabel's arm and tried to pull her back, but she didn't stop. Afam cast his eyes around, looking for an escape route when the man spoke out.

'What in the hell trouble have you got yourself into now, Belle?' he said, smiling an impossibly charming smile.

Annabel closed the gap between them and threw her arms around the man, pulling him into a tight hug. The man, David, returned the affection, placing one arm across Annabel's back, the other holding her head tight against his.

Annabel pulled back. 'David, this is the guy I was telling you about. He's the key to everything. Do you think we can help?'

'Afam, hi,' David took Afam's hand in a firm grip and shook enthusiastically, 'I'm David. Annabel's told me everything. Sorry that you've had such a rough time of everything. I've made a few calls on the way here. I think there's probably something we can do. Won't be easy, like, but nothing good ever was.'

Epilogue

Afam had been back in London for a few weeks before he got the chance to see David again. David had reserved a spot for them in his favourite Turkish Ocakbasi restaurant, Likya in Golder's Green. It was a place he always took new clients. People were more relaxed when they were eating, and Likya had a very easygoing atmosphere. The proprietor, Hasan, was a local legend — an incredibly warm character, he loved welcoming people to his restaurant and ensuring they had an excellent time. The place was always packed at the weekends, but mid-week it was slightly less busy, so was a great venue for conversation. Of course, it helped as well that the food was exceptional.

Afam had arrived before David, and Hasan greeted him warmly, showing him to a table tucked in the corner by the window.

'Can I get you anything to drink?' Hasan asked as he pulled out a chair for Afam to sit.

'Water, please,' Afam said, and Hasan walked off towards the counter, past rows of wine bottles arranged in wall nooks. He returned a few moments later and placed a glass of water in front of Afam, alongside a small curved glass filled with tea. Afam took a sip of the water and then stirred the tea using the small silver spoon sticking out the top of the glass. He lifted the cup to his lips and the scents of cinnamon, cloves and apple mingled with the bitter black tea in his sinuses.

Afam took a sip, winced as the boiling liquid scalded his lips and placed it back on the saucer. He dropped a sugar cube into the tea and stirred.

Afam had gone back to Lagos for Leye's funeral. Annabel and David had helped Afam repatriate the body, which had taken an extraordinary amount of paperwork and a not inconsiderable amount of cold, hard cash. David had forwarded some funds to help, with enough left over to put towards funeral costs.

It had been a strange experience, returning to the place he had called home for so many years. He was overjoyed to see his family again and had spent many long nights talking about his time in Paris, though he had skirted around the reality, presenting a palatable version of the truth. He had spoken of the tourist attractions, had told the anecdote of how he'd got his trial, which people lapped up, but when it came to details surrounding Leye's death he had kept quiet. The reality would be too hard to bear for his friends and family, and Leye's confession had brought him peace that he didn't want to shatter.

Leye's funeral had been sadder than Afam could have imagined. Police had traced Leye's mobile phone records and shown how he had entered the country, and the people he had been in contact with since he'd arrived, but the trail had gone cold. Investigators concluded Leye's shooting resulted from his involvement with criminal gangs. No arrests had been made — Leye had died in the ambulance. His family had buried him with no sense of closure.

After the funeral, Afam had stayed with his family in AJ City. He was surprised when he flopped down onto his old bed, that his room here was smaller even than the attic he had stayed in when he was in Paris. It had seemed huge to him back then, compared to what others had.

There was a knock on the door frame and Iman walked through the curtain that served as a door without waiting to be granted access.

'Hey.'

'Hey,' he replied, not moving from his prone position.

'Big day, huh?' she sat down next to Afam on the bed and flopped back next to him, the two of them staring up at the ceiling together.

'You could say that,' Afam said, keeping his eyes on the rusted tin roof.

'I'm sorry, Afam,' Iman carried on, 'I'm sorry about Leye. You know he meant a lot to me, too. I'm going to miss him. But I know you two were like brothers. I can't imagine how much you must be hurting.'

Afam took a moment to reply, 'It's okay, sis. Thank you.' He was trying not to be drawn into a conversation, but Iman wasn't letting him get away that easy.

'Everything okay, Afam? You've been acting strange. Stranger than usual,' Afam smiled at the jibe, 'I know you're hurting about Leye, but there's something else. I know it.'

Afam let out a long breath and closed his eyes.

'I...' he struggled to get the words out, though he didn't know why. He had gone over this conversation a thousand times in his head. Knew Iman would corner him. He loved her for it. 'It was me, Iman. It was me who killed Leye.'

He heard the breath catch in her chest and the eventual soft whisper of its release and turned his head to her. A tear rolled down Iman's cheek and she sniffed suddenly. Another intake of breath, she puffed out her cheeks and blew the air out.

'Tell me,' she said.

And so Afam told her everything, from the moment he had left the house that morning she had caught him, his trip to Europe, Awusi and Effia and Kojo, getting screwed by Isaac and his crew and then Leye finding him, trying to drag him into the gang, and their final confrontation that had ended up with Leye lying on the floor of an alley in a foreign city, his life slipping through his fingers.

'I can't stay, Iman. I can't stay and see everyone every day, lying to them, suspecting they know more. The woman who helped me, Annabel, she's hooked me up with her boyfriend — a football agent in London — and I'm going to go back there and talk to him. I have to do this, Iman. It's the only way I can make it up to everyone. I can't change the past. I can't bring Leye back. But I can try to make things right. Try to support his family.'

'I know, brother,' Iman said, eventually, 'I knew from the second I saw you again that you wouldn't stay. It's okay. You go. This isn't the first time we've been here, remember?'

Iman turned to her brother then.

'You don't need to destroy yourself over this, Afam. What happened with Leye was an accident. A horrible accident. You were both forced into an awful situation. It could have gone either way. I know Leye would say the same thing. He was a good boy, Afam. A good friend. He always wanted the best for you, wanted you to succeed. He wouldn't let you waste this chance. Honour him, Afam, go back to London. Just... not yet.'

She reached out an arm and wrapped her brother in a tight embrace. Afam sobbed quietly into his sister's shoulder, feeling the tension he had carried with him on the trip release. He would call Annabel in the morning and make arrangements to fly back to London in a few days.

* * *

'So,' David sauntered into the restaurant and broke the ice with ease. 'How did you get on back home? Nice to see the family I guess? How's your sister doing? Does she like her new school?'

Afam smiled at David, 'Loves it. She's fitting in nicely. She told me to thank you.' David and Annabel's generosity had not stopped at helping with Leye's funeral. After they had gone to the Nigerian embassy in Paris and negotiated a new passport for Afam, David had been in contact with some of the people who ran some of Nigeria's top football academies. In turn, they had connected him with some of their feeder schools and colleges and David had negotiated a scholarship place for Iman in a leading private school. All Afam's mother had to do was fund her travel. Afam ensured he was sending back enough to cover the expense, as well as buying her uniform and schoolbooks.

'Good! So, I have some great news — it looks like the club is interested. They want us to go down there next week for an introduction and to get you out on the pitch with the rest of the squad to see how you gel. It's a League Two team, which means you won't be buying your Ferrari yet, but it's a decent enough payday and the reality is you'll shine far and above the rest of the team. It won't be long before you're scouted for something bigger.'

'That is great news,' Afam said, parking thoughts of home for a while. The food they had ordered arrived, a toothsome mixture of grilled meats and meze: salty, tangy, chewy grilled halloumi, freshly made, delicately spiced falafel and a platter of soft, pillowy flatbreads and sauces. They shared the plates, tucking in with their hands and washing down the feast with more delicious apple tea.

'It will be a far sight different to what you did in Paris, I expect,' David laughed and Afam joined him. He felt lighter, since he had been in London, and the ground under his feet felt firmer. He had finally heard back from Awusi and she had updated him on how the family was doing. They had been taken into a women's refuge. It wasn't The Ritz, Awusi had said, but it was better than chancing it on the streets and in hostels as they had done for a few weeks after arriving in Italy. Now he had a legal passport, Afam had arranged to visit Awusi and the kids in a few weeks' time. No men could stay at the refuge, so they had arranged a weekend stay at a place by the beach. It wasn't much, but Afam hoped it would give the family a well-deserved rest, and would allow him to get to know them all a little better.

They went over the travel details and David gave more details about what Afam could expect from the trial. Once business was done, talk turned back once again to their personal lives. Afam felt remarkably comfortable around David. He knew a little of David's background, how David had grown from humble, working-class roots to get to where he was today, and it made him more willing to open himself up to him. He was a man of principle, and after their experience in Paris, he also trusted Annabel implicitly and therefore, David was trustworthy by proxy.

'Has Annabel had any more luck with her story?' Afam asked.

David rolled his eyes. 'Same old story there. She's working with the paper to get around the injunctions, but not having much luck. Her editor's livid about France. He's pulling out all the stops. I've been up against some of the most corrupt people in the sport, but this is another level. Full shut-down, cease and desist letters... We have to be careful. After what happened last time with the whole Anaia brothers scandal, there were some pretty serious threats.' David took a sip of the ayran Hasan had put on the table in front of him. 'There are some nasty pieces of work in this game. All we can do is try to come out on the side of good. The hope I suppose is that the supporters become more aware of this sort of thing and make a stand. That's what Annabel is trying to do. She's in Germany right now, following a couple of leads on the neo-Nazi thing in Dortmund. She's not just being belligerent for the sake of it, she wants to put the game back into the hands of the fans. That's what it's like in the lower leagues, but there's too much money in the game for it to not attract the wrong sort of people.'

Football was big business, Afam was learning. Far beyond the fans and the players lay a tangled web of unethical business practise, uncaring foreign investment and powerful lobbying. It was too vast for him to understand. All he knew how to do was play. And that was exactly what he would do.

He owed it to himself. To his family. To Leye.

Printed in Great Britain
by Amazon

16446070R00120